#Fangirlproblems

A Kpop Romance Book

#Fangirlproblems

A Kpop Romance Book

Jennie Bennett

To the girl who thinks she's not enough: it's okay to let people love you.

#Fangirlproblems

A K-pop Romance Book

Text © 2018 Jennie Bennett

Cover Design © 2018 Jennie Bennett

Cover Photo © Meet Cute Photography

Font © Sideshow and Cyreal

ISBN-10: 1982916419

ISBN-13: 978-1982916411

Editing by Precy Larkins

Printed in the United States of America

Contents

#fangirlproblem1

Feels. Too many of them. Most days, standing in a crowd for four hours sounds like an extreme form of torture, but not today. Today I'll see X-O in person. I've dreamt of this for years, and the time has finally come.

My Instagram is open to Chansol's latest picture, his dyed hair an unnatural red color that somehow makes him even hotter. He's wearing a striped shirt, leather jacket, and dark jeans. These are the same clothes I'd see him wearing when he landed here in Houston, my hometown. That thought alone keeps me on my feet.

I've left him a comment like I always do. *Can't wait to see you*, it says. While other fans are leaving comments about how much they love him, I'm always trying to write as if he were actually my friend and not a celebrity.

My username isn't anything exciting, either. @TalithaXO–my name and my favorite Kpop group.

My roommate and best friend, Samantha, took my profile picture. In it, I'm sitting in a field of bluebells, sunshine on my face. My short brown hair curled well that day, and I'm wearing my favorite round-framed glasses. It's one of my absolute favorite memories. One where I'm not just living day to day, but really living.

Jennie Bennett

Sometimes I wonder if Chansol ever reads my comments, but the likelihood is low. Today, however, I get to see him for real.

What if Chansol glances my way? Even the thought of eye contact has my heart rate up. He's going to be here soon.

Of course, that's only if the girl in front of me lets me look around her. Seriously, I didn't know they made phones that big, and she's holding it up like the apocalypse will occur if she misses filming a single second.

I'll forgive her since she's a fangirl. It's what fangirls do.

"Talitha," Samantha complains, rubbing her belly. "I'm starting to get hungry."

Bless her heart, she's come out with me when she's not even a Kpop fan. She claims her Vietnamese heritage is the thing that's holding her back from committing to Kpop. She thinks most of the men look too feminine for her. It's a major pet peeve of mine, but since I love her, I let it go.

"It should be soon, I prom–"

A huge cheer blasts from the multitude, cutting off my words. My bias is here. The thought shivers through my bones until it can no longer be contained. I join in the screams, jumping up and down so I can see.

Fangirl Problems

I'm submerged in the river of people, pushed along the current as everyone tries to get closer to the barrier. Curse my shortness. Most of the throng towers over my shabby five-foot-four-inch self. This can't happen. I have to see Chansol in person, at least once.

Because I'm willing to do whatever it takes, I use the advantage of my smallness to squeeze through places others can't. While the taller people are crowding forward by trying to step on each other, I duck down, snaking through all available holes until I'm front and center.

"Chansol!" I scream. I can't help it—he's here. I can't see him, but I know he's in the room and I want him to know I'm here, too. Doesn't matter if he'll never really see me. Knowing that he's heard my voice is enough.

Let's face it, Chansol is the bias that trumps every other bias in the history of ultimate biases. I've tried to branch out, to feel the same things I feel when I follow other groups, but no one makes me feel like Chansol does.

Six boys are heading down the walkway in sunglasses and hats, surrounded by a circle of bodyguards. I stop breathing.

Usually, I'm not that crazy of a fangirl. I mean, I've had my moments where I've squealed in front of a computer screen or gushed to my online friends, but it's nothing like this. The energy pounds, pushing into my soul until I feel like I'll go crazy if I don't let it out.

"Chansol!" I shout again.

Here they come, here they come, heretheyfreakingcome! I'm bouncing on my tiptoes to get a better view.

I can almost see Chansol's face. Those are his lanky legs, his long torso, and his—

"Kay!" Someone behind me shouts, ripping at my hair and pulling me away from the front.

My glasses slide crooked on my face, blurring my vision. I can't get them back on fast enough. In a flash, the boys are gone. Out the door, to their waiting cars.

No.

I missed them.

I didn't get to see Chansol's face.

My one hope in life is left ruined, thanks to another fangirl. Seriously, I've been living for this moment. I don't hate my work, but sometimes it feels like that's all I am. I'd like to be a woman, too.

I'm frozen, my hand still reaching out, hoping they'll come back. I waited almost five hours in a mass of bodies, and this is all I get?

The crowd thins around me, excited girls going home to get ready for the concert tomorrow. A concert I'm sadly going to miss.

I tried to save up the funds, but my car broke down right before tickets went on sale. Since I need a car to work, and a job to live, I had to hand over the cash to the mechanic instead of my bias.

The tickets sold out before I could get more money. Which is why it sucks to be an adult.

When I turned eighteen, I was so excited to move out and have a career. I applied for culinary school the second I could, moving into an apartment with Samantha. Now I wish I was still at home, saving my money. Maybe then I could do things like go to X-O concerts.

I'll have to take solace in the fact that my bias is in the same city as me. Or at least that's what I tell myself. Even if it's not good enough.

Maybe after the concert I'll wait for the boys to come out of the stadium. I can't give up when I know they're so near.

I might have a better chance of spotting him then, anyway. As long as I can convince Samantha to come with me again. I don't trust my driving skills that late at night.

"There you are," Samantha says, putting a hand on my shoulder and flipping me around. "You just abandoned me in the crowd of crazies."

"Sam," I say, my voice cracking. She may be my best friend and my roommate, but she doesn't understand my love for Kpop. There's no way she's feeling my pain.

She tugs at me again. "Let's get out of here. I feel like I'm going to get trampled."

"Not yet," I say. I want to sit and stare at the place where Chansol's feet walked a second before. Even if I didn't get to see him. "The traffic's going to be bad getting out of here, anyway."

It's true, and it leaves me a good reason to stay and wallow in my disappointment.

"I knew we should've taken a bus," Sam says, "but that's probably packed too. I can't believe this many people came out to see some weird Asian boy band."

I spin on her, the fangirl claws ready to come out. "Don't say stuff like that. Especially here. Or else you *will* get trampled."

Sam crosses her arms, popping a hip. "Yeah, I noticed they were a little nuts. That one girl totally knocked you over when they were walking by."

I know all too well, but I don't want to think about it.

"By the way," Sam says, "who was that tall one in the middle? He had a cute goofy smile on his face."

No. She cannot steal my bias. I had him first. Not cool.

"If you ever decide to actually listen to their music, I'll tell you."

Sam nudges me, a weird smirk on her face. I get the sense she's hiding something from me, but if she'd been listening to Kpop, I'd know it.

14

"Oh come on," Sam says. "You know I've heard all their songs."

I scoff. "When?"

"Every single day," she says, poking me in the shoulder, "when you're blasting it in your room."

I whack her hand away. "Ha-ha. Very funny." I'm not rolling my eyes, but it takes a considerable amount of self-restraint.

If only she knew just how much that missed moment has hurt me.

Jennie Bennett

#fangirlproblem2

The desire to live in another country. If I lived in Korea, this wouldn't be a problem. There would be fan events and concerts all the time.

Instead, I'm caught in the line of cars waiting to get out and with no memories of Chansol to relive later. Other than his torso. I guess I'm glad I got to see that for a moment, brief as it was. But this traffic isn't putting me in the most giving mood.

Sam and I are just sitting and waiting, so I pull out my phone to keep me entertained while we're not moving. Which is pretty much all we're doing.

"I don't know why I let you talk me into this," Sam says. "We've already been sitting here for half an hour."

"Because you love me," I say, putting on a fake smile.

Sam rolls her eyes. "Are we talking about that time you saved my life again?"

"Not to brag or anything," I say, "but saving your life is kind of a life altering thing. So yeah."

Samantha and I met in high school. I was helping out the lunch ladies one day and they asked me to get something out of storage from the school's roof. But when I got to the top, Sam was there, standing on the edge, ready to jump.

I took off my lunch lady gloves and did a silly dance to make her laugh, a dance Chansol did once when he was being interviewed. Sam and I have been inseparable ever since.

"Someday," she says, "I'll pay you back." Her head turns to look out the window and I swear I hear mumble something about paying me back soon, but it's so quiet I'm not sure if I heard her correctly.

We move an inch forward and my phone buzzes with a text. I close Snapchat and open the message from my co-worker, Jean.

Hey Talitha! How are you? Only people who want something from me start a text that way. *I was wondering if I could ask for a favor.* Bingo! *My boyfriend got free tickets to see Paramore tonight. Could you cover my shift?*

So many things wrong with this text, I don't even know where to start. First of all, did she have to rub her boyfriend in my face when I'm so painfully single? Second of all, how does she know I don't have anything going on? It's a Friday night after all, I could be...doing...stuff.

Oh gosh, I'm such a loser. All I ever do on a free Friday night is watch dramas and study Korean. Unless Sam forces me to one of her social gatherings where I spend all night huddled in the corner, afraid of people.

What time? I text back, because, really, it's probably better for me to work rather than sit at home wallowing in self-pity.

I bang the steering wheel. I shouldn't think about missing Chansol, because now I'm upset with myself. Sometimes Kpop ruins my life—but I can't stay away. It's something only a fangirl can understand.

The car inches forward a few more feet and I can finally see the exit. Looks like it's not so bad once we leave the lot. Thank goodness.

My phone buzzes again. 3:30

Crap. That's in an hour! It'll take me that long just to get to the hotel from the airport.

I shoot a quick reply. *I might be late, but I'll take it.* Jean owes me, big time.

"Change of plans," I say to Sam. "I have to go into work. Can you drive my car home?"

"You want me to drive this piece of junk?" Sam says.

I pet the dashboard. "Peppy is a nice car, you just have to treat him right."

"Whatever," Sam says. "I guess I can. How are you going to get home?"

I smile. "I'll find a ride with someone."

Sam bites at her cuticles. She does that whenever she's nervous. She hates driving Peppy. I don't blame her since the last time she did, it died in the middle of a busy intersection. This time though, it's fresh from the mechanic. She shouldn't have a problem.

"Is there an event tonight?" Sam asks, the side of her finger still in her mouth.

I work for a hotel catering business, so sometimes we do weddings and parties.

"No clue," I say. "I'm just taking Jean's shift."

"We need to get you a boyfriend," Sam says.

Does everyone have to rub that in my face? Sometimes I feel like dating any random guy I can find on the street, just so people would stop bugging me about it.

Sam drops her hand from her mouth. "What about Bryce?"

Oh, here we go. Now we're going to discuss potential mates for Talitha. No thank you.

"I'm not dating Bryce."

We need to leave this subject, pronto. I just don't know how to get out of it.

"Why not?" Sam asks. "Bryce was really nice to you that one time I met him."

Since Sam is like a Texas beauty queen who's never been date-less on a weekend, she wouldn't understand. Short girls with sneaker obsessions don't get guys that easily.

"Yeah, he's so nice he tried to feel me up while we were alone in the walk-in fridge. And he has a mole the size of a nickel on his right cheek—with hair growing out of it."

From the corner of my eye, I can see Sam cringe. "Okay, we'll strike Bryce off the list."

"List? Are you keeping track of potential boyfriends for me?"

"You weren't going to," Sam says, sounding annoyed, "so I had to take action."

Sam thinks she's doing me a favor, but she's not. All she's doing is making it harder. Because the truth is, the one thing I want more than anything is love. Real love. But I'm also terrified of it. I've been hurt by men before. Even my dad didn't want to stay with us.

"Is being single such a bad thing?" It can't all be awful. There has to be something that's better about being single. Oh! I know. "When was the last time you got ice cream without sharing it?"

I glance at Sam, who furrows her brow. "Eric just likes to try my flavor," she says in a small voice.

See? Singledom isn't all bad. I'm on a roll. "Don't you feel obligated to shave every day, too? I haven't shaved my legs in two weeks."

Sam hits me. "Talitha, that's gross. Don't even tell me that's a good reason for you to be single."

It is in my book. I should just go *au naturel* until a potential mate enters my line of vision. Which will probably be never, since the only guy I love is a mega

popstar who's mauled by fans everywhere he goes.

Jennie Bennett

#fangirlproblem3

Not wanting to live in reality.

The kitchen is the last place I want to be. I'm feeling a little queasy after wasting so much time and energy waiting to catch a glimpse of Chansol. The scent of chicken roasting assaults my senses, my stomach flipping over.

I'll have to man-up because I'm a chef and it's what I do. Food is my life.

"Talitha." Sherry, my boss, nods to me as I walk into the back to put on my chef's jacket and apron. That's the best greeting I'm going to get. She's not one for words, but I like that about her.

I pull the hair tie off my wrist and gather my dark locks in a ponytail at the base of my skull. One look in the mirror reminds me that I'm just an average girl, wearing average glasses, with average brown eyes, and a less-than-average height.

There's no point in daydreaming. Like Chansol would even consider dating someone like me when he can have any girl wants. In the world. Literally.

Maybe I should date Bryce. I can get over his mole. And his wandering hands.

I shake my head. No. It's too gross.

I wash until my knuckles are red, then take my station chopping peppers. There's nothing that centers me like slicing a knife through crisp veggies. It doesn't take long for my mind to go from boys to food. Who needs a boyfriend when cooking will calm the soul?

By the time the food is finished, I feel like a whole new person. Sherry even let me have a plate of Alfredo, and it was perfect. I love it when I get to serve perfect food to hungry people. Nothing's better.

It takes all five of us on the crew to set up in the small section of the ballroom. It's not that there's a ton of food, just that the warmers and trays are heavy. From what I gathered, we're feeding a small group of executives from another country, and they're only staying for three nights.

I envy them, getting to travel the world and eat amazing food. They're even staying in our five-star hotel. I could never afford to actually stay here.

When I'm done with culinary school, I'm going to try and find a job in Korea. I've been dying to learn how to make kimchi.

We're almost all set up when Sherry taps me on the shoulder. "Hey Talitha, Bryce's called in sick tonight."

Thank goodness, I didn't want to fight him off again. "Okay?"

"I think we're covered in the kitchen. Do you mind serving instead?"

"Sure," I say, 'cause it's what I do.

Hi, I'm Talitha. People ask me to help and I do it. I'm everyone's go-to man. Geez, I really love being walked all over.

I set down the platter of cheesecake I was working on and wipe my hands.

"Here's a uniform," Sherry says, handing me a pressed white shirt, vest, and a black bowtie. Whoopie! I get to look like a penguin.

My first task is to set the tables. It's a major pain, but the work dulls the emotions.

I kick open the swinging door from the kitchen, balancing the chilled salad plates in my hands. This section of the ballroom is amazing, all wood floors and velvety curtains, and there's even a stained-glass window.

I flex my fingers a few times after setting down the last plate, hoping it will warm my hands. It's my job to be as invisible as possible, but that doesn't stop me from taking a glimpse of the people we're serving. I'm halfway back to the kitchen when I slow my pace. I didn't notice at first—probably because I always think I'm seeing things related to Kpop—but this is no fluke.

My foot catches on a rug, and I stumble forward a little but don't fall. Walking is not good right now. In fact, it's downright dangerous. Because the people I'm serving aren't just executives from another country. Tonight, I'm feeding dinner to X-O.

Jennie Bennett

#fangirlproblem4

Always crossing the line from casual to awkward.

I spot Chansol first. He's taller than most people in the room and he's leaning against a wall, talking with Taehyun. Dangit, I'm not supposed to know their names. I'm not supposed to know their faces. I'm not supposed to fangirl in the middle of my job.

Still, I can't stop staring. My bias—the guy I love—is right here, in the room with me. It's so much better than I thought it would be. Maybe at the end of the night I can ask for one tiny signature. You know, in exchange for feeding them so well.

Chansol turns his head my way. I bet he felt me staring, and it's freaking embarrassing. My face flames up and I try to run out of the room, but my feet catch on the stupid rug again. This time I fall on my butt. Why do I have to be klutz right now? Bad timing.

Maybe Chansol's not looking. I don't dare glance to find out. All I can do is get up as fast as humanly possible and run from the room like a frightened mouse.

I can't go back to the kitchen. Not like this. I fan my face, pacing the halls.

Someone else can serve for me—there's no way I can be on top of my game. Not with Chansol here. But if someone else serves, I won't get the chance to see my bias up close.

I'll just have to suck it up and find some way to be professional. Holy crap, I need a minute.

I press my fists to my lips to keep the scream inside. Who cares if I'm missing their concert? I get to serve them dinner! I do a little hopping happy dance that causes my hair to fall out of my ponytail.

Shoot. I bet I look like crap right now. The law requires that I have my hair up, no choice there. Why didn't I think to bring my makeup with me, either? I really need to hide the dark circles under my eyes; my glasses only magnify them.

I run to the bathroom and try to fix what I can. It's no use, I look like a zombie. I give my hands another thorough scrub before heading back to the kitchen.

One breath in through the nose and out the mouth. Calm. Collected. Cool. Maybe not cool. I'm more of a derp than anything.

Sherry shoves the cream sauce in my hands before I can get in the door. I have to put this on the buffet table, stat. I find myself skittering back to the room with X-O. Even thinking about it has got me all aflutter.

Looks like I placed the last thing on the table. It's my job to make sure they're getting their food okay, so I step back as the manager and crew start to dig in. Chansol is still talking to Taehyun, and even though I'm not trying to look, I can see them glancing my way and whispering.

Professional. That's what I am, a total professional.

The fangirl beast is clawing at my insides, dying to break free, but I keep her caged. For now.

Chansol and Taehyun hang back, still whispering between their hands. What they don't know is how hard I've worked at my Korean, so I can pick out their words. I've been studying every night and chatting with strangers to improve my skills.

"Is it really that person?" Taehyun says.

I don't want to know who they're talking about. It'll only bring me heartache. I stand straighter, studying the wall behind their heads.

Taehyun pushes Chansol toward me, and our eyes lock. I forget to breathe. His eyebrows shoot up, his signature grin transforming his face. The grin that made me fall for him in the first place.

He looks like he wants to say something to me. I glance up and down the table, making sure we have plenty of food. I hope he's not upset with what we're serving.

My focus goes back to his face. The fangirl monster is banging at her cage.

"Have you ever heard of Kpop?" he says in English.

28

O-MO. Can he get any more adorable? I'm not sure how to respond. The monster knocks at my ribcage, ready to gush everything about X-O. But the sane side of me still has control. I can do this.

"Have you ever heard of water?" I say in Korean. "That's what Kpop is to me."

Okay, so fangirl monster had a little bit of say in my words. Mostly, I just hope I got everything right in Korean.

Chansol's brown eyes go wide. "Oh. You speak Korean?"

He actually seems impressed. Finally, my hard work is paying off. "Yes, I've been studying hard. Please accept me."

Taehyun leans around Chansol's shoulder. "*Daebak*."

See, Kpop isn't a total waste. Right now, it's saving me face, and maybe even making me feel a little cool.

"In fact," I say, hesitant to ask but knowing I would kick myself if all I did after meeting Chansol was say hello. "Could I get your autograph?"

"Stay here," Chansol says, putting his hands up then running to the back of the room.

Taehyun starts loading up his plate. Boy can eat.

Chansol returns, huffing. He hands me a picture with both of his hands. "Here."

It's a photo of him. All signed and everything. More than what I've asked for.

Sometimes my body starts doing stuff I didn't tell it to, because the feels attack tender places. I'm so touched he gave me this, so overwhelmed to be in the same room as him, so emotionally exhausted from everything today—I start crying.

Not just a tiny little tear dripping out of the corner of my eye, all cute and glistening. No, the snot hangs from my nose first. I cover my mouth as the salt water starts dripping across my cheeks.

The fangirl monster is free from her confines and has taken over my body. I'm a sodden, disgusting mess. There's no way I can stay here and have Chansol watch me being such an idiot.

#fangirlproblem 5

Sometimes I hate being a fangirl. It causes just as many problems as it does happiness.

I run out the back door to the garden and lean against the fence, letting the cries rip from my throat. I hold the picture above my head, so it doesn't get wet, and put my forearm across my eyes to try and quell the waterfall. It's messing up my glasses, but I don't care.

"Are you okay?" someone says—in Korean.

I sniff, looking up. Did Chansol follow me out here? Why would he do that? I dot at my face and my finger comes off with black flecks of mascara. Great. Now I bet I look like a raccoon.

My hand holding the picture slowly comes down. "I'm fine," I say, even though I'm not.

I'm starting to think I liked it better when Chansol had never seen me. Then he wouldn't know what an embarrassing, emotional mess I am. Especially when it comes to him. It's the most ridiculous thing. I should be excited. Shouting from the rooftops. Dancing in the street. But I really wanted my time with Chansol to be perfect.

Being a perfectionist might make me a great chef, but it also gives me serious anxiety, which is now manifesting in the form of more tears.

"I promise I'm not that awful," he says, a hint of his beautiful smile raising the corners of his mouth.

He doesn't understand what he does to me. I don't even know if I can put it into words. All I know is when I see him, something stirs inside me. It's like hurricane-force ocean waves are crashing in my stomach, knocking me around and messing with my sense of judgment.

"I'm sorry," I say. I might as well be honest with him. I've already shown him just how insane I am. It's not like I'll ever see him again.

If I get it all out, then I can move forward with my life and he can forget me. Heaven knows I'm totally unworthy of his attention.

Now the problem is finding the right words. Korean is my third language—after English and Spanish—so it's not as easy to express myself. "I've just...admired you for so long. It's stupid, I know."

Why does he have to look at me like that? His round eyes are searching my face, his expression too serious. "That's not stupid at all."

He rubs one finger under the collar of his shirt, like he's uncomfortable. "Just...don't cry over me. I'm human, same as you."

As if I don't know that. His life is so public, I feel like I've seen all sides of him. There's not much he can do to hide it.

"That's what I like about you," I respond. "You're human."

His hand drops. "Really?" The word comes out as a whisper. Like he doesn't believe me.

I can't imagine that. He has to know how attractive he is. There are girls screaming his name on a daily basis. He does something as simple as eating and it drives everyone wild. How can he not know?

My finger runs along the edge of the picture. "I actually like you the best when you're making silly faces and cracking cheesy jokes."

There it is. That amazing smile girls line up to pay and see. I'm getting it for free. It almost doesn't feel fair that I have a moment with him like this to always remember when so many others want to take my place. I can't count the number of fans he has. It's almost... Overdone.

I snort at my own Kpop joke, the title of one of X-O's songs. I have got to spend less time on the Internet.

He takes a step closer, and I freeze. "What's so funny?"

Oh boy, I can't even begin to explain my thought process to him. "It's nothing."

Another step.

I backpedal into the fence behind me. Why is he getting closer to me like that? It's unnerving.

"Tell me," he says. "I like funny."

33

Don't I know it. But my joke is so corny, no one should be forced to listen to it. Plus, I'm pretty sure Chansol doesn't think in Kpop the same way I do.

"No really, it's stupid."

Another step. "Tell me."

Is this his form of torture? Because it's working. "No. Just...let it go."

One more step. I have nowhere to run. He's going to touch me in a little bit if I'm not careful. I want it, but I'm afraid of it, too. What if it's not as good as I've been wishing it in my head?

"You have me curious," he says. "You can't leave me hanging."

I need to deflect. Fast.

"I was just...thinking about you," I say, the first thing in my head plopping out of my mouth. Idiot. At least I didn't mention I was thinking about his lips. I'm sure kissing is the furthest thing from his mind.

He places a hand on the fence behind me, leaning in. "What about me?"

I cannot handle how close he is right now. Holy crap, I can smell him. It's sweet and spicy, like cinnamon sugar. I should've known he'd smell that way. It fits his personality. It's also making my mouth water.

"Um..." *Quick—Brain, think of something clever.* "You're so beautiful when you smile."

Brain, you've betrayed me. I didn't ask you to say whatever you were thinking, I asked you to be clever.

"And that made you laugh?"

Now he's inching forward, breaking my personal bubble.

"Not that, exactly," I say, trying to backtrack. I can't even remember what I laughed about now.

His other hand lands on my other side, trapping me under him. "Then what?"

Meltdown! Meltdown! Nuclear collapse to commence in three...two...

"I don't... I...You see...I–"

My mouth snaps closed as a sudden racket sounds from the ballroom. I crane my neck to see shadows through the windows. At least twice as many people are inside as before.

Bright lights are flashing, blinding even through the glass.

"Paparazzi," I say in English. I have no idea how to say that in Korean.

His eyes narrow, head tilting to the side.

I slip out from the box his arms created, so he's forced to turn.

It looks like an assault inside. My co-workers are in there. All of X-O is, too. I start toward the door, but Chansol catches my sleeve and spins me around.

35

"We have to get out of here," he says.

We? We don't even exist on the same plane. Besides, I'd hate for anyone to get hurt when I can help. My face is still toward the door. "But...what about them?"

"This isn't their first brawl with the media." That's true. Why didn't I think of that? "It's more dangerous for you if they see us together."

He has a point. As many fangirls as I've known and loved, there are a lot of crazies in the mix. All it would take is ten minutes on Twitter, and I can find a handful of girls who think their *oppas* belong to them—and they would go nuts if any other girl came near.

"Come on," I say. "I know a secret way out of the hotel."

#fangirlproblem6

Not letting my fantasies overtake my truth.

I had this dream once. Chansol and I were stuck on a deserted island, and he was in love with me. We lived happily ever after.

Never have I woken up smiling, but that day, my cheeks hurt from stretching them so far. I have to keep reminding myself that this is not that dream. This is me trying to save my idol's reputation. I wouldn't want him ruined over someone as inconsequential as me.

I feel bad I have to take him to the front of the hotel this way, but there's nothing else to be done. We're huddled side by side against the building, our arms touching, so we're not exposed through the windows. It's a blind spot, and no one can see us unless they came right upon us.

His body heat seeps through my clothes, gooseflesh erupting on my skin. *Not a dream*, I keep reminding myself, so I don't get caught up thinking this is anything more than an escape attempt.

My hands wrap around the picture he gave me, holding it to my chest. I'm grateful that at least I have this, and the memory of him, because it's time to let go.

"Behind those bushes, there's a fence," I whisper, releasing one finger to point while turning my head to see him. "It's a tight squeeze between the building and a brick wall. And there's a tree in the way. But it will get you out front and to safety."

"You're coming with me, right?" he says.

I work to keep a straight face, but inside I'm freaking out. This is totally something Chansol would say in that dream where we're together. Only, it would be because he wanted me romantically, not because I'm helping him escape.

"I think it'll be safer if you go alone." I manage an even tone, despite all the wobbling happening in my stomach. "What if there's more paparazzi out front?"

"That's exactly why I need you," he returns.

I press his autographed photo even closer to my chest. Anything to keep my heart from leaping out of my ribcage.

"What do you mean?" I ask, because I'm still living in that dream where Chansol needs me to be his girl. Even though I'm not.

He's still so uncomfortably close to me. Yes, we're hiding, but that doesn't change what he's doing to my body. It's hard to think with him next to me.

"You know your way around this hotel," he says. "If there's more trouble, you can save me."

Right. I'm just the employee and he's the celebrity. He needs my knowledge, not me.

"Of course," I say. "Yes, I'll go with you."

I'm still surprised how easy the Korean is coming to me, and how much I understand him. I mean, I've done well in my practice with my Korean teacher, but I never thought I was this good.

I feel his shoulders relax. "I'll give you a boost over the fence," he says. "Since I'm taller."

Yes, he's six feet and I'm a lot shorter, but it wouldn't be the first time I've scaled that fence.

"Let me show you how it's done," I say. I need my hands free, but I'm not losing this picture. I tuck it into the back of my pants and under my shirt to protect it. Then, I run.

The rocks scatter under my feet, but I find enough grip to propel myself forward and take a giant leap, clinging to the top of the fence.

My arm scrapes on the tree bark, but I use the trunk to get a foothold strong enough to propel me over the fence and to the other side. My feet ache and I'm a little scratched, but I did it.

"That was brilliant!" Chansol yells. I can picture his stupid giddy face. Goodness, he's too much.

"Shhh," I say, finger to my mouth. "They'll hear you."

"Right," he says, lowering his tone. "I'll be right over."

I turn around to get out of his way, but he's faster than I expect him to be. He leaps over the fence with so much force, there's nothing I can do to retreat.

He rams into my side and both of us trip. We're spinning and tumbling toward the ground. He's aware enough of the situation that he presses my head into his chest and turns us as we're about to hit, so my weight lands on him.

My glasses fly off to who knows where. He grunts as we land, no doubt the air pushed from his lungs.

Great. I've just bruised my favorite idol.

#fangirlproblem7

Never knowing when to stop.

I try to get off him as fast as I can, but his arms tighten around me.

"Don't shift your weight," he says. "It hurts."

I close my eyes and inhale, so I can hold my breath. He's not clinging to me because he likes me. He's doing it because he's injured. Goodness, though, he smells good.

"Yeah," he says, his voice breathy. "Just...go slow."

I press my hands to the ground on either side of him, lifting myself straight up. If my vision wasn't so horrible, I would be able to see his beautiful face instead of the blur in front of me. I'm practically blind without my glasses.

Careful not to touch him again, I lift one side of my body and flip toward my back, landing in the rocks beside him. The picture is still tucked into my pants, but I can tell it's gotten wrinkled in the action.

I take a moment to breathe then get to my feet to hunt for my glasses.

"Does it hurt very much?" I ask as I begin my search.

"I'll be fine in a minute," he answers. "What are you doing?"

"I lost my glasses. Do you see—" *Crunch.*

Crap.

I hear a light laugh from Chansol. "They're under your foot."

"Thanks, Sherlock," I answer, sarcastic. I lift my shoe as gingerly as I can, but I'm wearing high-quality sneakers since I'm on my feet for long hours. There's only rock under where my glasses were. It's not a pretty sight.

I pick up my glasses—one side is swinging in the breeze, and as I try to put them on, it breaks off. A lens is missing, and the other has cracks through it. At least I can see out of that one eye, crooked glasses or not.

The sound of scattering rocks alerts me to Chansol's movement. I turn around to face him.

He slaps a hand over his mouth as he snorts.

I must look like a freaking dummy right now. I rip the glasses off my face, but then regret it as soon as I do. I have to be able to see.

Screw it. I've come this far. It's not like he first spotted me wearing Cinderella's gown. I came in as the servant girl wearing her tattered clothes with soot on her face. Then I cried. Broken glasses? That's nothing.

I put them back on, chin held high. My eyes narrow as I dare him to laugh.

This time, he doesn't utter a sound, only shifts his weight, focus on the ground.

"You're hurt," I say, my voice softening as I step toward him, pointing at the blood on his neck.

He cups the wound, looking surprised when his hand comes away red. I approach him, placing my sleeve over the blood. "You have to put pressure on it, this is a bad place to be cut."

I lift my face to find him staring into my eyes. I've lost my freaking mind. What makes me think I can stride up to Chansol and touch his neck? I wasn't thinking about the person, only the injury.

Stepping back, I notice it's only a nick that's already slowing. He covers the injury with his own sleeve.

I clear my throat, trying to focus. How much more of this can I take? This isn't just any guy, he's *the* guy. The one I would do anything for, and it hurts to know he'll never feel that way for me.

"I'll go ahead," I say. "You stay here while I check if there are more paparazzi out front."

He nods, still not raising his gaze.

I clomp forward, keeping behind a tree near the front corner of the building. It's worse than I feared.

Media vans crowd the entire half circle. People with microphones and cameras are hanging around, waiting to get a shot. Crap, something huge must've happened to cause this firestorm.

"Doesn't look so good," Chansol says, sneaking up on me.

I jump, screaming and throwing a hand over my heart.

He's right behind me, that stupid grin on his stupid pretty face.

"You scared me," I pant.

"Sorry," he says, putting some distance between us. "I wanted to see what you were seeing."

"What are we going to do?" I'm not really asking him, more like the universe. Maybe I can sneak him back into the hotel and he can hole up in his room.

"I can't stay here," he says, as if reading my thoughts. "If it's this bad out front, I'm sure reporters are all over the hotel."

He's right. Which leaves us with nothing.

"Maybe," he continues, "you know of a place where I can lay low for the night?"

There are two places with where I spend my time: home, and here. "I don't know..." I lift my head to look in his eyes. "There are plenty of other hotels around here."

He empties his pockets. "I don't have any money, or a phone."

I can't afford a hotel room for him, and my purse is inside, anyway. I would have to face the madness to get it. I could, but that would mean leaving Chansol alone and vulnerable.

"How were you planning on getting home?" he asks, his tone measured.

Why would he worry about me? I'm a nobody. "I was going to hitch a ride with one of my co-workers," I say, realizing that isn't going to work out anymore.

He nods to himself. "I have an idea."

"What's that?" I ask, afraid to hear the answer.

He smirks. "If you can create a distraction, I can grab our van. I know where they've attached the spare key."

I give him a full-on smile. I know exactly what I'm going to do.

Jennie Bennett

#fangirlproblem 8

Thinking I know what I'm doing, when really, I'm just moving forward through the darkness.

"As soon as I go out there," I say, "You make a run for the parking garage. It has two exits, so make sure you take the one to the highway."

"Got it."

I take off my broken glasses and put them in my shirt pocket, hating that I won't be able to see, but also knowing how suspicious it would look for me to be wearing them.

"Here goes nothing," I say aloud, facing forward.

It's a good thing I know the basic outline of the hotel's front lawn, because I can't see the reporters from this distance.

I pause at one of the bushes out front and pretend to pick something off it. I have the advantage of wearing a hotel uniform, so maybe they'll think I came from the back because I work here.

After messing with that for a minute, I casually stroll across the lawn. At least I hope it looks casual, because the urge to put my hands forward and feel my way across the lawn is strong, but I refrain.

As I get closer, I can make out the outline of the reporters. Thank goodness I went the right direction.

46

"Excuse me," I say, approaching them. "What are you all here for?"

I have no idea if I'm talking to the right kind of person or not—this is a disaster.

"We're here for X-O," someone to my right says. "The Korean boy band."

"Oh!" I say, nodding. "I saw those guys earlier."

A bunch of blurry people crowd around me, all of them with thick Asian accents. At least they're speaking English, so I don't have to reveal my Korean. It's amazing that reporters would follow these guys to the other side of the globe. "Did you see the tallest one?" someone asks. "Does he really have a girlfriend?" another says.

Crap. Are they here because they heard Chansol has a girlfriend? If he does, that would make me the sucker of the century. Not that I really thought he was single. I'm sure I imagined that spark between us. He's too handsome to be available, anyway.

"Does he have red hair?" I ask the reporters. I can't really tell, but I think I have their attention now. I hope Chansol is making his escape while they're focused on me. "I think I saw him in the back when I was getting into the garden shed. I can show you."

"Please do," someone says, but as soon as I turn, someone else latches onto my shoulder, stopping me.

"No, we need her as a witness. Send someone else to check out her story."

Crap. I guess I won't be meeting Chansol at the highway. I hope he makes his escape and doesn't wait around. I should've told him to just go. I can find another way home.

"Did you see a girl with him?" one reporter asks me. I turn to her. "How did he look?"

I keep my mouth shut.

"I'm Nana, by the way," she says, reaching out a hand. I don't take it. "Strange he wasn't in the ballroom with everyone else, isn't it?"

Who does this girl think she is? I hate that they're using him this way. Why can't they let him live?

"He looked like a person," I respond. "And he was alone."

Nana doesn't quit her gossip. "He must've been back there to meet someone. I heard Tina is in the country, I wonder if it's her."

Tina of Generation Girl? The most popular girl group in Korea? That would totally make sense. She would be someone worthy of Chansol. More worthy than me, a humble fan.

I'm not sure if it's the bright lights, all the people crowding around me, or the fact that I can't see, but my breath is hitching in my chest, palms sweaty.

48

My knees get weak, and I start to crumble. This was a bad idea. I'm not cut out for this. Shouts snap my attention back to the present moment, the roar of an engine scattering people.

"Is that Chansol?" I hear someone say.

I whip out my glasses, rushing to put them on. Chansol has the passage door open, a mask over the lower half of his face and a cap low over his eyes. There's no way they could prove it's him with picture proof, not with his entire face covered.

"Get in!" Chansol screams. He didn't follow the plan. Instead of heading for the highway and escaping, he came back for me, almost plowing straight through the reporters to get here. But they're recovering as fast as I am. If I don't run now, they'll catch Chansol.

Jennie Bennett

#fangirlproblem 9

Feeling indebted to my idol for existing.

I run, taking Chansol's lead and covering my face. I knock away cameras and people to get to that waiting passenger seat. Chansol takes off before I have the chance to close the door, and I have to heft it with all my strength as Chansol plows into oncoming traffic. More horns blare as he cuts people off with the huge van, burning rubber in his haste.

My seatbelt isn't buckling quick enough. I didn't know Chansol could be this crazy. I pull the picture out of my back while I'm at it, but it's too late, it's already been ruined. Maybe I'll have a chance to get another one.

"There's someone on our tail," he says.

I cling to the handle above the door until I can no longer feel my fingers. "Why did you come this way? You were almost free."

"I couldn't abandon you," he answers.

I'm about to ask why, but I scream instead as he shoots through a red light, almost getting us t-boned.

"Are you trying to die?"

He makes a hard left, glancing in the mirror as he goes. "I'm saving your butt, you could thank me."

I want to—really, I do. I can't number the times I've been grateful just to watch his music videos and live streams. I wish I could tell him all the times he'd comforted me when I was feeling down, but somehow this seems like the wrong place.

We have to lose these paparazzi creeps first. The freeway ahead gives me an idea. Texas is somewhat unique in their freeway system. Feeder roads run parallel to the freeway, and everyone merges and exits onto those roads. The only way to turn around is to get off, take the feeder to the next light, and go around a U-bend under the freeway.

But here's the kicker that might save us: the turns are blind to what's happening on the other side and there's plenty of shops along the freeway. Chansol would have to cross three lanes of traffic and abruptly pull into a parking lot, and then step on it until he's behind a building—but the paparazzi are far enough behind I think we can pull it off.

"Get on that road!" I say, grabbing the steering wheel.

"The freeway? Are you crazy?" he asks.

"Yes. Don't merge on, take the U-turn."

He shakes his head but steps on the gas.

"Don't slow down as you take the bend," I caution. "As soon as you get around, pull into the parking lot."

He does as I say, almost hitting a car in the far lane.

"Step on it, get behind that building!"

Jennie Bennett

This might be a huge lumbering vehicle, but with Chansol behind the wheel it really goes. The van squeals behind a building, stopping so fast that I thrust my hands onto the dash to catch myself.

We wait. Both silent and breathing heavily.

"Do you think we lost them?" I say after a couple of quiet minutes.

"Let's wait a little longer," he replies.

The longer we sit, the more my defenses ease.

"I guess I should thank you now," I say. "I thought I was about to faint with all of those people around me."

He slides his hands down the steering wheel as his shoulders relax. "It's no problem. I was the one who broke your glasses, so I should help."

I shake my head. "What if they took pictures of us?" Honestly, I created that distraction so Chansol could escape and no one would see us together. Him coming back for me makes no sense at all.

He leans his head into the seat. "I only did it because I found the mask and hat. It would be hard for them to get a good shot of my face. Plus, I'm pretty sure your back was to them, and I took off too fast for anything to be in real focus. It won't be enough evidence to convince anyone."

I let out a long breath, my worries going with it. "So, what are you going to do now?"

He glances at me, lowering his mask. "I didn't get to finish my dinner, and I'm hungry. Maybe we could find a phone and I can see how the guys are doing?"

Neither of us have money or phones. But there is one place he can contact people. My apartment.

"We could," I start, feeling nervous. "I mean if you don't mind...maybe you could come to my pla—"

"Yes," he says before I've even finished the word. He looks suspiciously happy about it.

"Okay, then," I say with a shrug, "my place it is."

I have to remind myself that this means nothing. I'm just helping him out. But man, does it feel like it's more. The only thing I know for sure is, Sam's going to kill me for not telling her.

Jennie Bennett

#fangirlproblem10

I wish there was a way to magically know how to react around your bias.

Chansol's going to see my apartment. It doesn't feel real. Having him sitting next to me in the van, smiling his signature smile...it keeps confusing me.

The blood on his neck is dried and flaking off, which shouldn't be hot. But it is. It matches the crazy color of his hair. Goodness, he's handsome.

I want to say something to him, anything. Under pressure, my Korean came easily. Now I have the chance to get to know him personally, but the only word floating around in my head is *michesseo*. Which means, *are you crazy?* Because I am. I'm absolutely insane to let Chansol come to my house.

This isn't going to work. Space. That's what I need. What if I get attached?

Scratch that—I'm already attached. I've been attached for so long, loving him every day from a distance. But this is different. He's been looking at me, interacting with me, even touching me.

I feel so dang guilty. I took him away from his bandmates. If I hadn't cried and left the room, he never would've followed. Why couldn't I just be normal and say thank you?

He didn't have to follow me, though. I still don't understand why he did. Then he took it a step further and saved me. There has to be a deeper reason. He's met hundreds of fans in person. Given out high fives and signed pictures like they cost nothing.

The airport this morning was a good example. So many fans were gathered, hoping to see him—maybe even touch him—but he didn't give them a second look. Broken glasses or not, he wasn't obligated to come for me.

I want to dig and figure it all out, but I'm not sure how.

"Do they have music in America?" he says, breaking the silence.

What kind of question is that? Of course they have music here. How else would I know who he is?

He's smiling like he just told the best joke ever. Now I get it. He wants me to turn the radio on.

Immediately, Taylor Swift or some other overplayed, overly adored artist booms through the car. Although, it does have a catchy tune. After a second, I start to bob my head.

All right, maybe I'm getting into the beat. Just a touch.

It builds to the chorus, and I start singing before I'm even aware of what's happening, my shoulders shaking to the sound.

My teeth clack as I shut my mouth. I only sang, like, one line. There's no way he heard me. How could I get so lost as to forget Chansol is sitting beside me?

He keeps turning his head to look at me. I swear he's laughing.

"Shut up," I say, swatting him. Stinker.

The chorus comes around again and Chansol clears his throat.

My heart drops as he starts to sing along. He doesn't sing often in X-O, but when he does, it surprises me. It only takes three words for me to realize he's better than he thinks he is, which is saying something.

He's bouncing along to the beat, his legs getting into the motion. "Sing!" he yells when there's a break in the lyrics.

Well, if he's going to make me... I start soft, but he shoves my shoulder. "Louder." Since his voice is drowning out the radio, he probably can't hear me too well. I decide to do as the song commands and *Shake It Off*.

We both start belting, laughing at the music. It's so cheesy, but I like it at the same time.

When the song's over, we're both cracking up so hard my stomach hurts. It feels good to let go.

"You're coming to the concert, right?" he asks.

I look down at my lap then back to the window. I don't want to tell him no, but doubt I can get tickets this late even if I had the money. I'm going to the venue, though. I have to at least try something.

"Yeah," I say, giving him my half-truth.

He beams, looking way too happy. "You're going to love it," he says. "You'll be so surprised."

Surprised? Why do I feel like he's talking about me in particular and not just the concert goers? I can't puzzle it out.

"Hey," he says, nudging me out of my reverie. "You're really cute when you're concentrating like that, but you don't have to overthink it."

The last thing I want to do when I'm trapped in a car with Chansol is blush, but my face heats to a million degrees, unbidden. I thought I was supposed to be in control of my emotions.

I can't take it any longer. He has to know how much this thing—whatever it is—is killing me. I can't live in my dreams forever, and if we're going to spend more time together, I might as well draw a line.

"Don't say stuff like that," I groan.

Even though there's still music in the background, the silence between us becomes awkward. I don't know if I have the guts to express everything I'm feeling, so I leave it at that.

"Why?" he asks, tentative.

I chew at my bottom lip. What can I say that will satisfy him but not reveal my true feelings? "Because...we can't be friends." That should work, right? He's an idol, and I'm me. If we're friends, I might get hungry for more. I already am hungry for more.

"And why can't we be friends?"

Dangit, how do I answer? I wish I hadn't started this conversation. My gaze turns to the window, so I don't have to see his face.

"I know you," I say. "You're nice to everyone. You have a positive attitude about life. Even when you're trying to avoid the paparazzi, you thought about me before anyone else. But that can hurt you. I'm afraid of what other fans might do. If you're friends with me, it might cause you problems later."

He needs to leave me as fast as possible so the pain in my chest can stop. It will throb less once he's gone.

"Funny," he says, a smile in his voice. "You don't think I can take care of myself?"

I swing around so I can see his expression. He has a half-smile and not a care in the world.

I roll my eyes. "I'm not saying that. I'm just saying I'm your fan. Nothing more. It was dangerous for you to approach me. I could've been a *sasaeng*."

"But you're not," he says, reaching across the space the separates us and taking my hand. "I can tell the difference."

Well, that backfired. The heat in my face increases until I feel my ears burning. Is he really holding my hand? I know in Korea it's common for friends to hold hands, and I'm sure he's just trying to comfort me. It's working. A little.

"Look," he continues, as if it's no big deal that our fingers are interlocked. "It was my choice to follow you outside. It's my choice to be here, and it's my choice to be your friend. You can respect that, can't you?"

Of course I can. It's just that it's ripping me apart to have him so close knowing I can't hold on.

"Sure," I say, anyway.

"Good," he responds, relaxing enough that he starts driving with one hand. "Let's try this again. You have a beautiful smile."

He's really not going to give up. I guess if I get this time with him now, I should take advantage.

"What, like this?" I say, flashing him all my pearly whites.

He nudges my shoulder. "Yes. Like that."

It's so hard to be mad at him. He's just too cute.

"How's your neck feeling?" I ask, releasing his hand and leaning across the middle console to get a better look.

He stiffens. "It's fine." I swear his voice went up a pitch.

I reach out one finger to touch the wound. It looks like it'll heal clean, at least.

"I should've gotten out of the way."

"No," he says. "I should've been looking out for you."

I scoot back to my side, continuing my study of the landscape passing by. It's all splintered because of my cracked glasses. "I guess I owe you for saving me."

"Yep," he says, not missing a beat. "You do. I'm going to have to think of some way you can repay me."

Holy crap, that's just an expression. Like I could ever repay Chansol for everything he's done for me.

I'm dying to know what he's thinking, but I'm afraid at the same time. "What did you have in mind?"

"Hm," he says, his chin getting all wrinkled as he thinks. "A coupon."

He wants twenty cents off yogurt? "Coupon?"

He nods, his face bright. "Yeah. A coupon book. You know—wash my car, cook me a meal..." He clears his throat. "Free hugs. Stuff like that." He said the last words way too fast, but I got it. He wants a free hug, eh? I'd make him a giant book of free hugs if he asked for them.

60

The only problem is, he'll never use them because his stay is temporary. I guess it doesn't hurt to entertain. "If that's what you want."

His grin almost reaches his ears. "It's what I want."

Gosh, he's beautiful. I can't get over it, no matter how much I try. It's not just the way he looks, it's that he causes everyone around him to feel his energy. I can't stay upset in his presence, no matter what. He has all of me, whether or not he wants it.

I search through the glove box and find a scrap of paper and a pen. FREE HUG, I write in English. I stuff the coupon in his shirt pocket and sit back, pleased. I hope he uses it sometime soon.

"This is our exit," I say. I don't want to say that because it means we'll sleep in separate rooms and then he'll go in the morning. And when he leaves, my heart will go with him.

#fangirlproblem11

Too much time on the Internet=an unprepared fangirl in an emergency.

The lighting in my apartment hallway is shabby at best. It's casting a green glow over Chansol. I'm sure I look deader than Frankenstein's monster. I'm only staying in this light because there's a community phone in the hallway, and I want to make sure Chansol calls the hotel and lets everyone know he's safe.

If things have died down, he can go back. In fact, it might be better for him to go late at night. I guess I'll find out if he's leaving soon or not.

He tries to push me into my apartment, but there's no way I'm going to abandon him.

I can hear the phone ringing on the other end, but only faintly. Chansol has his back against the wall and he's smiling at me.

My hand goes through my hair again, and I keep wiping under my eyes hoping to remove any traces of mascara. Like that's going to work. I wish he would quit staring. Yeah, I'm a mess, but he's making me feel super self-conscious about it.

"Hello?" Chansol says, standing taller and turning around.

I can hear some angry Korean on the other side.

"I'm sorry," Chansol says. "It just worked out that way."

More angry Korean. Someone's asking if he's crazy—among other choice words. But Chansol is patient—he listens to everything and waits until whoever he called has calmed down enough so he can speak.

"Yes, I'm fine," I hear him say, eventually. He gives the other person my address and apartment number, since I had to give it to him to get here. Then he says something I don't understand. "The whisk...it's here." His back is to me, but he keeps glancing over his shoulder. He lowers his voice. "So, you know, if you could help with that."

With a whisk? I don't get it.

"Thanks, I owe you," Chansol says, hanging up the phone.

Weird way to end a conversation.

"Is everything okay?" I ask.

Chansol pulls out his full-force smile. "Yep. Should we go?"

I hand him my keys. "You clean up first, then we'll eat. I have some phone calls to make, too."

Chansol grips the keys in his hand but doesn't make a move to leave. "You waited for me. I'll wait for you."

I call Sherry first to let her know why I left work and that I'm safe. She tells me to take the weekend off and recover. I know that means less money, but my mental health is important here.

Sam is next on my list, since she's not in the apartment when I checked a minute ago. "Finally!" Sam says when she hears my voice. "Do you know how worried I was? I called, like, twenty times."

"I'm sorry, I—"

"Forget it," Sam says. "Your car broke down. Again."

No! I really can't afford more repairs right now. And I definitely can't afford a new car. "What did you do?"

"My dad came to help me. I'm going to be staying at home tonight. Your car is in my parent's driveway."

Freaking fantastic. I don't have a source of income the next few days, so I won't be fixing it anytime soon. Looks like I get to take public transportation for a while. Wa-hoo. Not.

I tell Sam goodbye and slam the phone back in the hook. I spin on my heel to see Chansol with his hands in his pockets, his lips a straight line. I guess even if he didn't understand what I was saying, he can sense the tone.

"Sorry," I say, tucking some of my brown hair behind my ear.

The sides of his mouth rise in a closed-lip smile. "I'm just worried about you."

I take off my broken glasses and rub the bridge of my nose. He shouldn't be worried about me. He shouldn't even know who I am. So many girls would die to be alone with Chansol, but all it's doing is hurting me. Knowing it won't last—and feeling closer to him by the second—it's not right.

"Let's go get washed up," I say, walking ahead. Both of us are covered in dirt from the hotel, and I feel like a shower will make us new people. I don't really want to cook for him in the state I'm in.

I get to my door before I remember I gave him the keys. Instead of telling me to move like any sane person would, Chansol puts one arm on the frame opposite the doorknob so I can't escape before unlocking with his left hand.

I'm looking at his face, because he's so close. I already knew he had an amazing profile, but this proximity is a whole new experience. I've never taken note of the way his jawline swoops up to his ears, or how his hair curls at the base of his neck...until now. Not even pictures could pick up that kind of detail.

The door opens, and I stumble back, my sneaker heel catching on the entryway. Chansol grabs me before I fall, his bicep strong against my back, and his face centimeters from mine.

Oh no, this is exactly the type of thing I don't want to happen. His eyes lock in on my face, searching every inch.

I try to turn my head, but it's like my neck doesn't work. All I can do is stare back.

Dang, I want to kiss him.

Everything is amazing—the way his arm feels, the sound of his voice, the shape of his torso. A hurricane builds inside me, wind and rain pounding on my heart, ocean waves stirring my middle. My fingers are tingling, legs trembling. My whole body is aware of his nearness. It shakes me until I don't have any confidence in my ability to stay away.

One moment passes, and I know I can't let him go anytime soon. I've been fighting it, but now I'm in enemy territory. If he leaves, it'll tear me in two. I didn't want it to be like this. I wanted to enjoy loving him from a distance and not knowing the real him.

I need to give him my trust, but my experience cautions me to keep the walls up. My own father made me so many broken promises. All it took was a few lonely birthdays for me to know the mistake was on my part for believing him. No one has ever fought for me, and I feel like an idiot for allowing even the smallest part of Chansol in.

Because I know he'll break my heart. Everyone does. And Chansol is the big pop star with a life so much better than mine. The ending is obvious before it begins, but now that I'm in this deep there's nothing I can do. Only prepare myself for the eventual explosion.

That last thought shakes me awake. I spin out from his arms, tripping as fast as I can to the other side of the room.

"The bathroom's right there," I say, pointing at the door. He doesn't have extra clothes, but he can wash his face and hands. Or he can put on the same clothes he had on before.

I'm not sure how clean the bathroom is, but since Sam's a neat-freak, it can't be too terrible.

He keeps shifting his weight, scratching at the back of his head. "You should go first." His words feel unsettled.

"It's okay," I say. "You have to leave soon, and I live here, so..."

He lets out a breath of a laugh, stretching an arm. "Yeah...that's actually why you should go first. I'd rather clean up at the hotel."

I guess I can understand why he'd be uncomfortable, but I hate to think he's leaving that soon. What if he just *goes* while I'm in the shower?

"You..." I start. I really shouldn't be saying this, but I can't leave him alone in this room if I won't ever see him again. "You'll say goodbye before you go, right?"

He nods, smiling. "Of course I will."

Jennie Bennett

I'm sure I'm being obvious, but I can't hold it in. I like him, okay? It's not like it's news in my life. I like him and I'm alone with him, so I should use the short time we have together.

I run to my room and gather my stuff, determined to take the fastest shower in the history of showering. I also have an extra pair of glasses, thank goodness.

As I shut the bathroom door, I catch him watching me. I want to dance, it feels so good.

It takes too long for the water to get warm, too long for me to scrub and shave, too long to get dressed and put on a little makeup.

I want to show him that I don't always look like an undead person. I even grabbed a cute lacy top and put on my skinniest jeans.

There's not much I can do about my wet hair. I don't want to waste time blow-drying, so I get it as dry as I can with a towel then throw in some gel so it's all curly. My old glasses have thick black frames, but not as huge as the ones Chansol normally wears. They look okay. I like my other glasses because they're not as noticeable.

Chansol stands as I open the bathroom door, a huge smile crossing his face. I smile too, feeling shy.

"Wow," he says in English. He's looking me up and down. I almost feel like he wants me to spin around.

Now I'm embarrassed. Even though I was trying to impress him, I didn't expect him to actually notice.

I point to the bathroom door, trying to deflect the attention off me. "Are you sure you don't want to clean up?"

He licks his lips once. He has no idea what that does to me. Even covered in dirt and blood, he's still sexy.

"Actually," he says, "that sounds nice."

I get the suspicion he was only putting off cleaning up for me, not because he wanted to go back to his hotel. I guess it's already done, but I'm upset I didn't pick up on it.

Before I can say anything, he slides past me into the bathroom. I already hear water running by the time I think about asking him what he wants to eat. I don't want to assume he likes anything, and I've don't have Korean food lying around.

Instead, I put my clothes away in my room. I really want to tidy something else to ease the nerves, but it looks like Sam did a deep clean earlier today.

I spot my laptop neatly put away next to the table and my fangirl instincts take over. I haven't been online for, like, four hours. I'll just check things online real quick.

Sure enough, the second I open Twitter I have thirty-five notifications. I start giggling as I go through each one. People have been tagging me in pictures of Chansol. It's kinda funny to see him all dolled up when I've just spent the last few hours with a dirty and dingy version of the same thing.

There are articles, too. No doubt the ones that sent the paparazzi to the hotel. Rumors of Chansol dating. I ignore them.

Before I know it, I'm lost in the void. Maybe it's because Chansol's in the next room, but I'm especially squealy tonight. I don't tell any of my friends what's actually happened. Not while Chansol is still here. Besides, without picture proof, none of them would believe me. There're too many liars on the Internet as it is.

Maybe I can ask Chansol for one *selca* before he goes.

I land on a particularly handsome photo of him I haven't saved to my computer and start the downloading process.

"Anything interesting?" Chansol says, leaning over my shoulder.

I jump and shut my laptop in one motion. Did he just catch me drooling over him online? My head turns so I can judge his expression—but instead, I end up falling out of my chair.

Chansol, the sexiest guy on earth, has just been standing over me with his shirt off.

#fangirlproblem12

Sometimes, it's impossible to suppress the perv.

Chansol has a beautiful face. I like everything about it, even his big floppy ears. I should be looking in his eyes and focusing on his words, but he's standing half naked in front of me, which makes it hard to concentrate.

"Sorry," he says. "I decided to take a shower. But my shirt was ripped. My coat is okay, but I didn't know what else to do."

I hear all the words. I understand them totally. I just can't seem to take action. He flexes a little—I'm sure it's an accident—but holy moly.

He bends down so his face enters my vision. I'm pretty sure I'm drooling.

"Do you have something I could wear?"

I should definitely get him something to wear. This shirtless thing is not going to work for me. I'm totally paralyzed by his beauty. I wonder if we could take that *selca* now.

He waves a hand in front of my face. "Talitha?"

When did I tell him my name? I don't remember introducing myself. Maybe I did. Everything's a blur.

I blink. A shirt, right. I'm not sure I have anything big enough. He's really tall and lanky, but it's not like he doesn't have muscle. Because I'm looking. His muscles aren't in question.

"Um," I stutter, still having a hard time focusing on his face. "I think I have an oversized hoodie."

It's oversized for me, at least.

"Lead the way," he says, moving one of his arms.

How could such a little gesture make me so crazy? I'm absolutely nuts right now. It's too much to be with him like this. I better find that hoodie fast.

My feet don't work that well when my brain is rattled. I tear my eyes off his amazing abs and wobble over to the front closet. Hoodie...hoodie... It's a boy's L, so it should do the trick, hopefully.

I stay in the closet and hold out the sweater with pinched fingers like it's dangerous. If I turn around to look, it'll all be over.

He takes it from me. "Are you going to stay in there all night?" he says a second later.

Does that mean he's dressed? I turn around to see his nakedness covered, thank goodness. I was having way too many inappropriate thoughts a second ago. All right, I still am.

He reaches a hand behind his head to do a nervous-neck-scratch thing and a little of his skin shows right above his jeans. That's way worse than him being bare-chested.

I flip around to close the closet door, but I'm not thinking right, so my head smacks into the doorjamb.

His hands grip my arms to keep me from falling, again. When did I become a klutz? It wasn't that long ago when I was vaulting over the fence.

"Are you okay?"

No. I'm not okay. I'm a walking embarrassment.

"Yeah," I say, afraid to let him see just how vulnerable I am.

He leads me to the couch and sits me down, one of his arms still around me. "Let me see," he says, moving my hand from my forehead.

Now that I've given in and let myself feel—now that I know I'm attached—it's too much to have him so close. He's real, he's in my life for the moment, and I'm already going to be heartbroken when he goes.

I jump up, spinning around and taking my first proper look at him since he got out of the shower. Crap, he was in my shower. I wonder if he touched my loofah.

Focus.

"Do you know when you might leave?"

I need to prepare myself for the time when I'm going to be ruined.

"Uh," he says, scratching under his good ear. "I think it'll be a while. Taehyun said they're still looking for me so..."

Is he saying he's going to stick around? The urge to keep my hands busy surfaces again.

"What do you want to eat?" I say, clapping my hands together.

He gives me another of his signature smile. "Anything."

Okay, that's a tall order, but maybe I can figure something out. Not to brag, but I'm an awesome cook. I mean, I'm going to culinary school—it's a given.

If I had planned ahead of time, I would've gotten a good cut of beef or expensive fish. I open the fridge and rummage through the options. I do have some rice, premade. I could throw veggies in it and make a stir fry, but I won't. It seems too cliché to feed to an Asian.

The vegetable drawer gives me a better idea. I pull out some peppers, mushrooms, and onions. If there's one food that's universally liked, it's eggs. The cheese comes out next, some sliced ham, and of course, the rice. Rice in an omelet is killer good.

I dump the ingredients on the little bit of counter I have then start searching for a cutting board.

When I stand, Chansol's in my personal space. I step away, flattening myself against the counter, caught off guard. If this keeps happening, I might die from a heart attack.

#fangirlproblem13

Never being satisfied.

"Anything I can help with?" he says, attitude still bright.

Mouth-to-mouth resuscitation for my lost breath? "I think I got it," I say. Honestly, I don't like to be bothered in the kitchen. Him standing here is torturing me enough.

He picks up a pepper. "I'm pretty good at chopping."

I laugh. I can't help it. Lots of people think they're pretty good at chopping. They're not. Knowing how much Chansol's been babied by his eating schedule, I'm sure he's not even close to good.

"Really, I can handle it."

He points to the eggs. "I can mix those up."

There's no way he knows what it takes to mix eggs to perfection. He hasn't seen me get started yet.

"No," I say, flat out. "Just let me handle it."

He folds his arms. "What can I do then?"

I look around my little four-by-four kitchen. "Hm, you can stand there and look handsome." I feel a little self-conscious for being so forward, but he caught me online looking at him—I have nothing to hide. Not to mention the way I reacted to meeting him in person. He's gotta know I think he's the most attractive man on the planet.

I can see my words make him even happier. A happy Chansol is the best Chansol.

He stands next to the pantry. "Here?"

I nod as I tie an apron around my waist. "Perfect."

"You sure you don't want to chop things side by side?"

Flirting? I swear, Chansol was just flirting with me. My heart is going a million miles an hour.

I shove him a little, just to show how much I liked him getting his flirt on. Because any excuse to touch him is a good excuse. I mean, if he's sticking around I should take advantage. I'll worry about the pain tomorrow.

Lucky for me, the only counter space big enough to chop is right next to where I placed Chansol. I get lost slicing the veggies, grating the cheese, and cracking the eggs.

Oil's been heating in a pan, so I throw in the crisp peppers and onions to soften them up a bit. I add some garlic too, because garlic is the best smell when you're hungry. Gets the mouth salivating.

I start another pan with melting butter and whisk the eggs with milk until it's an even yellow color.

If this omelet is going to be perfect, it has to be seasoned just right. Everything else can be fine, but if you add too much salt—it's over.

There's nothing like fresh cracked pepper in eggs, so I reach for that next.

The pepper grinder is on the second-to-the-top shelf, right above Chansol's head. I set down my whisk and wipe my hands on the apron.

Why did Sam think it would be a good idea to put the pepper out of my reach? I'm pretty sure the stool is in the bedroom—I needed it this morning to get my favorite jacket out of the top of the closet. Guess that means I'm going to jump for it.

This kitchen is so small. When I get to the shelf, Chansol doesn't have the space to move, which puts me halfway against his torso. Even though I feel his warmth through his shirt, even though I can smell the cinnamon-sugar sent wafting off his body, I don't stop reaching. I'm determined to make this the best omelet he's ever had. Each time I jump, I get a little higher, my fingers grazing the wood.

Missed again. One more jump and I should—

Chansol catches me around the waist with one arm, stopping my motion. My knees are touching his legs.

Blood flushes to my heart, my skin goosebumping. With his other hand, he reaches behind him and pulls down the pepper. I make a grab for it, but he places it on the counter instead.

"Talitha," he says in a serious tone, and I raise my gaze from our feet to his face.

Bad idea. Dark puppy-dog eyes are digging straight into my insides. I don't have secrets anymore. Chansol's eyes can see right through me.

Without saying a word, he knows exactly how crazy I am about him.

I try to back away, but he has me tight. "Coupon," he says, pulling out my FREE HUG card and setting it next to the pepper.

Now? It's probably good I turned everything to a low heat, but still.

His other arm wraps around me, holding me captive. I know I owe him an embrace, but I can't bring myself to move my arms from my side.

My culinary reflexes are screaming to lean forward and grab that stupid grinder, but Chansol's face has me captivated.

He nods toward the shelf. "Anything else you need me to get?"

All the food ideas I had a second ago are gone. Flown straight out of my brain. The only thing I notice is Chansol's perfect mouth. I swallow, not daring to leave, but also not daring to stay.

"No. I—"

He cuts me off with a kiss, his hands pressing into my spine. That perfect mouth—lips I've admired for so long—have made contact with mine. His fingers dig into my back as he lifts me up, so he doesn't have to bend down so far.

I don't understand how this is happening. I'm just his fan. I've done nothing to deserve this, even if I've been wishing for it forever.

Half of me thinks I'm so unworthy I need to run the other direction, but the other half is in the moment, where my mouth is moving to the rhythm of Chansol's. His breath is sweet and spicy, just like him—a cinnamon tang that fills my nose and makes my mouth water.

Finally, I allow myself to realize he's not leaving anytime soon, and I sure as heck am not going to be the one to end this kiss.

My trembling fingers dare to touch his sides. At first, I just grip the edges of his sweater, but the more we kiss, the braver I get. My hands splay across his back, pressing him closer to me until his abs are right against my chest.

Chansol picks me up and swings me around, setting me on the counter and knocking all the food away. Now his face is leveled with mine, our lips synchronizing as our heads turn, noses brushing.

His breath tickles my skin as he steps back for some air. We're both panting, and my lips feel swollen.

He gives me another soft kiss, and I lean forward for more, hungry for his touch.

"Wait," Chansol says, not stepping back but not kissing me, either.

Our lips aren't touching, but the tingle of energy lingers between us.

Chansol closes his eyes and I feel his desire this time. He wants to kiss me again, and I want to be kissed.

"We should stop," he says, but then he tips his chin up so our mouths meet again.

This time my hands go around his neck, his strong shoulder muscles flexing under my arms. His fingers wander across my back, pulling me closer until our bodies are flushed.

I take one deep inhale, and then lean away—breaking the kiss. Chansol stumbles forward, surprised at the sudden stop. I have to duck my head to the side to keep him from kissing me again.

"The eggs!"

Chansol sniffs so he smells it, too. Burnt oil, burnt vegetables, burnt eggs, ruined omelets.

I slide off the counter and run to the stove. It's a black disaster.

"Crap," I yell, turning off the burners as fast as I can.

Everything's a mess. This was supposed to be perfect.

My eyes prick with tears. Chansol kissed me. I don't know why, but it can't be because he likes me. It was just that I was close. And here.

Men are like that anyway, right? They see an opportunity and they go for it. He doesn't know how much his absence will kill me. I don't want this to be a one-night stand kind of thing.

I'm falling for him. Not just as an idol—or even the person I've admired for so long. I like the man that's in front of me. The one who saved me, took care of me, and kissed me so passionately I could've sworn he loved me too.

The tears continue to prick at me as I scrape the burnt eggs into the sink. I haven't done one smart thing since I came face to face with him, but this takes the cake for the worst of them all.

It's over. I don't even know what I'm doing, thinking I could cook for him. Like that would make a difference in the course of our lives. He's an idol—he can't stay with me.

"I should go to my room," I say, my back turned to him. It'll be easier to let him go if I don't have to watch it. "I'll order you some food first."

There's a pizza place close by and I have my credit card on file for their website.

All I know right now is that a knife is stuck in my heart and he has the power to twist it and kill me, or pull it out and let it bleed. Either way, I'm damaged for life.

Jennie Bennett

#fangirlproblem14

There's no separating the fangirl from the emotions.

With my head hung low, I start retreating.

Chansol puts his arms around me, pulling me into his chest in a back hug. "It's okay," he says. "I'll stick around for a while."

I twirl around–breaking his grip–my vision fuzzy with tears. That kiss was too amazing. His arms around me feel too good. The sound of his soothing voice does too many things to my soul.

"A while?" I say, backing away until I'm in the living room. Distance. "What are you even doing here, really?"

I need to know, because each second I spend with him becomes more tainted.

"Talitha." Even the sound of my name on his lips is overwhelming. "It's not what you think."

What does that mean? Is it because he knows what a weakness he is to me? Does he understand how much it hurts knowing it can't last? Because right now, I feel like he's taking advantage of my feelings for some physical pleasure.

"Then what?" I say. "Any second, Taehyun will call and I'll never see you again. Dammit, Chansol, I care about you. This can't be some fling. Not for me."

"I know," he says, pulling at the sides of his hair.

I scoff. He knows? If he really knew, he never would've followed me outside. If he understood what the simple act of him being near me does, he wouldn't have tortured me this way.

I wait, arms folded and eyebrows raised.

"No one's calling me," he says.

I'm not sure I heard that right. If I did, that would mean he actually wants to stay here— which doesn't make sense. "I'm sorry?"

He smiles. "I told them not to bug me. The concert's been pushed back a day because of the media, and—"

"Hang on." I have to stop him because I need to understand what he's saying.

So, he wasn't honest about someone coming to get him, and he's been making excuses ever since we got here. I'm not even sure if anything he said was one-hundred-percent truth.

I should forgive him for lying. I should be ecstatic because he did all those things to spend more time with me, but I don't get why he needed to do it that way.

One look at him and those big dark eyes melt me. How can I hate him when he's so beautiful? I can't just let it go, though; he needs to understand.

"There's something I don't think you get," I say. "It's great that you're staying. I want you to stay. But it's not enough. That kiss—" I have to stop because I'm choking up. It's hard to talk about what just happened because I want to pretend it was a dream.

I only imagined feeling his hands all over me. Only envisioned being so close to him we were practically one person.

"That kiss," I say again, the lump in my throat making it hard to talk, "is just a tease. It's a reminder of what I'll never have. I'd rather not be close to you. I don't want to spend time with you if it's going to end. It's better if you go now, so I don't fall deeper. You mean too much to me."

He doesn't have any more excuses, I've laid it all out there.

I don't know what I expect—him to walk away, maybe? But he doesn't do that.

His head is down, so I can't read his expression, but he's not moving and he's not saying anything. He lets out a sigh.

"It doesn't have to end," he says, his eyes meeting mine in an attempt to pierce straight through my brain.

But it does. I knew it before I even met him in person.

With two long strides, he crosses the room to where I am. His hands cup my chin, pulling me up to his face. He kisses me before I'm aware of what's happening.

He slides a finger right underneath my ear, still holding my face in his hands. It takes willpower I didn't know I possessed to not lean into him. "I meant that kiss, and I mean this one, too," he says.

His hands are warm on my jaw, his words drawing me to him, his lips begging me to meet him in the middle.

I give in.

There's nothing like this kiss. It's Christmas morning, and my birthday, and an X-O comeback all rolled into one. It must be a new year, too, because fireworks are exploding in my chest.

Resistance? Ha! Resisting when he's closed the space between us is impossible. I'm still afraid. More afraid than I've ever been, but if he's serious, I have to forget that.

I'm grateful to have him in my arms, period. It doesn't matter what he says, there's no guarantee he can stay. Now. This moment. It's all we have. I can't ruin it any longer. Not if he doesn't want me to.

It's because I care. Because of my feelings, I'll give him peace. For the moment, anyway.

Tender kisses on supple skin makes my heart melt and my senses open. He guides me to the couch, sitting me down and tangling his fingers in my hair. I grip his waist, but the too-small hoodie keeps pulling up so my fingers are touching skin.

It's amazing being kissed like this. It's almost as if I'm the only one he wants. He's the only one I want too, which is why I have to be careful.

"We shouldn't," I say in between smooches, but I'm not committed enough to pull away.

He holds my mouth captive one more time, pulling away slowly. Moisture causes our lips to stick as he lets me go.

"Everything okay?" he says.

He kisses me once more like he's still not done. I know how he feels. "We can't go too far," I say, my voice breathy.

His lips come again, heavy on my mouth. "You're right."

He's so good at ruining me, but I'm starting to get serious. "Yeah. I mean, I want you—"

I shouldn't have said that because now he's kissing right under my ear, both his hands roving across my back. Ugh! Why does he have to make this so hard?

"Chansol, stop."

He breaks the embrace the moment I command it, sitting on the other side of the couch, far away from me.

I didn't want that much space, but maybe it's better this way.

"I just want it to be special," I say, reaching over and taking his fingers. "If," and I mean *if* because I still don't think this can work, "if this is going to last, I want to save the best part for later. When we know we can be together longer."

He nods, but he's not looking at me. Oh crap. I made him mad. I don't want him mad, but I'm sure taking things too far would be a mistake right now.

There has to be something I can do to make up for it, and I have a feeling kissing isn't going to be the solution. Even if I'd like it to be.

What we really need is a change in pace.

I stand up. "You're probably still hungry. How about we finally get that food?"

Jennie Bennett

#fangirlproblem15

The simplest things make me happy.

Even world class chefs have to order pizza when the circumstances call for it. Chansol and I share an orange while we wait for the delivery, talking about his favorite music.

"I was surprised when you had Coldplay on your Instagram. I've liked them for a long time, so it made me feel closer to you."

He peels off an orange slice and shoves the whole thing in his mouth—only chewing a couple of times before swallowing. "I'm sorry about earlier," he says. "You were right about us stopping. I just needed a minute to calm down."

That was random.

"I really like you, so it was hard," he says.

He really likes me? It's still hard for me to comprehend, but he was the one who said the words.

Dangit, now I want to kiss the smirk off his face. "I wasn't worried about it."

Is he blushing? He's been so open with me I didn't think his shy side would come out, but here it is in full view. I like it.

"What I'm curious about," I say, feeling devious, "is how much you like me."

There's an orange slice in his mouth and I watch him swallow the thing whole. That's gotta hurt. He gulps a few times then takes a drink of water. "You don't know? I didn't show you well enough?"

Holy crap, he's being serious. He actually likes me. It's not that he kissed me because we're alone together, it's because he likes me. Enough to stop kissing me when I asked him to.

Yep. This has got to be a dream.

The doorbell rings, and I pay the delivery dude my entire jar of change since I'm feeling nice. Even if I don't have enough money to fix my car.

"Should we watch a movie?" I say, sliding the hot pizza on the table.

"Sure."

I pull out my laptop and the picture I was saving is still on my screen. I close it as fast as I can, hoping he didn't notice but knowing he did. When I dare to peek at his expression, that signature smile is so wide I'm afraid his face will break.

I try to think of all the Korean movies I've wanted to watch. It should be something he understands, too.

"How about this one?" I say pointing to a picture of two very attractive guys, not that that's the reason I want to watch.

"No way!" he says, a little more forcefully than he needs to. "*Pororo*. Let's watch *Pororo*."

Isn't that a little kids' show? I giggle but pull it up, anyway. It's my one night with him, I don't care what we watch.

It's getting really late. Or really early. Either way, I'm exhausted. After one episode I can't sit in the hard kitchen chair anymore.

I'm not really sure what to do about sleeping arrangements, because I know if I invite him into my room it'll be trouble. But I can't offer him Sam's room, and I can't let him sleep on our hard couch.

"You can sleep on my bed," I say. "I'll just sleep out here."

He gives me a look that says don't-even-think-about-it. I give a look back that says what's-your-solution-genius?

"How about this," he replies. "We spread some blankets on the floor and we both sleep out here."

Man, he really doesn't want to let me go. But that sounds just as dangerous as the bedroom.

He seems to be thinking about it too. "We should sleep head to toe."

Yeah, I know I'm not strong enough to resist him spooning me in the middle of the night. It'd be better if his feet are in my face.

"Deal."

I grab every blanket we have in the house like we're building a fort. Before long, we're lying down, drifting to sleep.

"Talitha," Chansol says, right before I fly off to dreamland.

"Hm?"

"I'm really glad I got to meet you today."

Seems strange that it's only been a day, but I'm grateful for it. "I'm glad too," I say. It's hard to think when I'm tired.

"Talitha," he says one more time.

My eyes are heavy, but if he wants to talk, I'll always listen. "Yes?"

"This isn't the end. Don't give up on me."

Jennie Bennett

#fangirlproblem16

It's harder to let myself be loved, because I'm a fangirl.

The pain starts in my heart. It's a pinprick in my chest, a needle stuck through my skin all the way to my wing bone. Everything convulses and contracts, erratic with agony.

Chansol. I want to say his name out loud, but I can only focus on the throbbing.

"Don't," I manage to squeak out. But it's all wrong, too filled with the hurt.

Remembering is the hardest thing. Remembering what it was like to hold him, and smell him, and kiss him.

"Talitha."

I even have his voice echoing around my head.

"Talitha."

The sting spreads from my chest to my stomach. It hurts. It hurts everywhere.

"Hey, wake up. Talitha, are you okay?"

I startle, sitting up and clutching my chest. It was a dream. All my fears coming through while I slept.

His cold hands press into my cheeks. "Talitha?"

I can't focus on him without my glasses, but he's real, and he's sticking around.

"Are you okay?" he asks again. "I'm worried."

I pull my glasses on, wanting to make sure it's really him. "How are you here?"

He smiles. Gosh, he kills me. "I drove you here last night. Remember?"

I do, but it still feels dream-like.

His hand trails down my neck and to my shoulder. "I think you had a nightmare."

Did I? Is that why I feel a cold sweat on my brow? "It was so real. You left."

He plays with my hair, tucking a piece behind my ear. "Nope. You have to keep dealing with me, at least for a while longer."

As if this isn't my fantasy come to life.

"You know," he says, his wandering hand trailing down my arm. "You look really beautiful when you first wake up."

I automatically cover my face, realizing how horrid I must appear. Morning breath, too. Ugh.

He eases my fingers away from my eyes. "I want to take a good look at you."

"I'm ugly."

"Never," he says, kissing my forehead.

This is the best dream I've ever had. But it can't be a dream, because I really have to pee and my stomach is growling.

Chansol's hands start wandering again—around my shoulders, down my arms, up into my hair. Never mind my own physical needs, I can't stop looking at him.

Every place he touches is fire. I might as well burn into a crisp right now for all the touching he's doing.

His face leans closer, and I can tell he's going to kiss me again, morning breath be damned.

That, I won't tolerate. I want Chansol to remember me as sweeter than the aftertaste of pizza.

I roll out from under him and find my feet. "Sorry," I say, walking backward. "I'll just…" I point to the bathroom with my thumbs, and then I run.

Pull yourself together, Talitha. He's still here and he's obviously still into me. Heaven knows why.

It would be so easy to just give in and let him hold me, but I need to be stronger than that. My nightmare wasn't just a dream, it was a premonition of things to come. All I can do is be strong while he's still around.

I do the best I can to clean myself up in a short amount of time, then come back out to the living area.

Chansol has neatly folded our bedding and set it on the couch. I don't see him, so I walk into the kitchen. There he is, all one hundred and eighty-five centimeters of him. Half of his hair is pushed straight up, and he still has a sleepy face on.

He's doing the dishes, as if this reality couldn't get any better.

"You don't have to," I say, running over and trying to take the pan from his grip.

He grins wide. "I'm your guest. I wanted to."

"But–"

He puts the pan in the drying rack and shakes the excess water from his hands. "You're too late, I'm already done."

Not fair. I haven't been able to do anything for him yet.

"Chansol–" I start with a sigh, but a loud knock at the door cuts me off.

I raise an eyebrow, and he shrugs. Crap. What if his manager is here to pick him up? We just started talking. I'm not ready.

No one can take him if I don't open the door. I look out the peephole and see a manager standing there. Not Chansol's manager, but mine. The building manager, that is. I didn't call for him, and I know my rent is paid.

I wrench the door open, biting my lip. I hope Chansol stays in the kitchen. There's no way of knowing how the building manager will react to a boy in my place. Technically, I can. As long as he doesn't move in with me. But it's better to be safe. I'd rather avoid the questions.

"Can I help you?" I say softly.

"There's a phone call for you in the hall."

I try not to let my relief show. "Great, I'll just take it then."

The building manager heads down the stairs, and I pick up the hanging receiver. "Hello?"

"Talitha!" It's Sam. She sounds flustered. "Have you looked outside yet?"

"No." The view is better inside my apartment at the moment.

Sam huffs. "Well, I can't make it back this morning. The roads are insane. It's raining really hard."

Heat rises to my face. I shouldn't be blushing, but I hope this means Chansol and I are rained in. I still don't think we should do *that*, but it'll be nice to have him around.

I twist the phone cord around my finger. "Is it?"

"Dangit!" Sam says. "I'm the worst friend ever. You're all alone. I should be there for you."

I forgot she doesn't know Chansol's here. I don't want to tell her. It'll ruin the fantasy.

"It's fine, really. I have plenty of food, and I've been wanting to try making something new, anyway."

I can almost *see* Sam pouting when she speaks again. "Are you sure?"

"Have a nice day with your family. Call Eric. I'll enjoy my time alone, I promise."

"Fine," she says, biting, "but I'm coming back the second I can."

"I love yooooouuuuu," I say as I move the phone away from my ear and hang up. I'm glad to know she cares, and also glad she's not coming back yet.

When I enter the apartment, Chansol's at the table dangling a slice of cold pizza over his mouth.

My legs are too dang short. "No!" I scream, running. "Don't eat it!"

I jump onto the table trying to get up high enough to knock the pizza out of his hand. He takes a gigantic bite, unaware of my attempt.

"I wanted to make breakfast," I say, laying out on the table, defeated.

He stands, setting down the slice. Crap. I don't like the look in his eye. He leans over me, placing a hand on either side of my shoulders. It takes him a second to swallow, but he never takes his eyes off mine.

"I only had one bite," he says. "You can make me breakfast, if you want."

How can he still smell like cinnamon sugar? I thought after a shower and sleeping...but no.

I should say something. It wasn't my intention to be pinned under Chansol like this. I just like cooking, and I wanted my food to be the first thing he ate this morning.

My arms pull into my chest as I tuck and roll off the table. Chansol laughs as I bowl over the chairs on the other side of him. I end up falling less gracefully than I planned. My feet can't find purchase as I scramble up, so I use the table edge for support to stand.

"Am I that scary?" he says once I've composed myself.

Yes, he is. Terrifying. I can't trust myself around him. "New rule while we're stuck here. Three feet distance. The length of this table."

He folds his arms, his mouth turning into a thin line. It sounds dumb now that it's hanging in the air, but I'd like to get to know the real him, not just the physical side. I've only seen who he is in front of the cameras.

I hold my hands up as I step around the table and toward the kitchen. "Three feet."

He looks like he's trying to hold in a laugh, but I don't let that deter me. I grab a spatula and hold it out like a weapon. "You just stay right there while I cook."

His demeanor collapses as he scoffs. "I'll comply, but only until after breakfast."

I suppose that's acceptable. "You better."

His hands go in his hoodie pockets—my hoodie pockets—as he smirks. "It's probably good, anyway. You have me feeling all kinds of things. Mostly nerves."

Me? No way. I don't know what I could possibly do to him to make him say that. Not to mention how bold he's been with me. If this is nervous, I'd wonder what his comfortable looks like.

I let the spatula drop to my side, the burning question that's been in the back of my mind finally rising to the surface. "Chansol, why are you here?" I mean, I know he's here because of the media, but there's something else. "It doesn't make sense that you'd stay with me like this. Are you sure it's okay?"

There's that neck-rub thing he does so sexily, again. "Talitha, you have no idea. When SM approved my idea to come here—" he cuts himself off, looking at the ground. "Look. It doesn't make sense now, but it will. Tomorrow night. If you want me to leave until then, I'll go. I never meant to force myself on you."

SM approved his idea to come here? As much as I want to know more about his statement, I decide he needs to understand how much I don't want him to leave.

"It's not like that. I want you here. Promise."

I love how his ears lift when he really smiles. There's so much adorableness, I don't know how he can contain it all.

He claps his hands together. "Glad we got that out of the way. Now, what are you making me for breakfast?"

Jennie Bennett

#fangirlproblem 17

Finding laughter in unlikely places.

The Dutch pancakes are still steaming when I place them on the table. I wanted to make Chansol something that he maybe hadn't tried before.

"What's this?" he says, his eyes going wide.

When I said pancakes, I'm sure he was expecting something flat that could be flipped to cook both sides. That's not how Dutch pancakes work. They're more like an egg-bread cake. They even bake in the oven and rise.

They also have a perfect pocket in the middle for fruit or whatever else. Today, I stick with the traditional lemon juice and powdered sugar. It's not too sweet, and I love it.

"Just cut it with your fork and knife, then dig in."

I wait for him to eat first. My favorite part of being a chef is seeing someone enjoy their meal. He lifts his fork as if he's proposing a toast, then shoves it into his mouth.

His jaw works as he takes the first chew, and I hold my breath, knowing the flavor's going to hit him any second. At first, his nose scrunches, his eyebrows folding inward. His mouth pinches as he swallows. He turns his head, coughing into his arm, and then takes a giant gulp of milk.

Was it really that bad? I cut my own bite and let it swirl around my tongue. It's fantastic. Soft in the middle,

100

crispy on the outside, with a hint of citrus. The powdered sugar has melted into the bread so it tastes like frosting.

When I look up, Chansol has his hand in front of his lips. His eyes are slits, like he's smiling so huge he might burst. He snorts, and I try to reach over the table to smack him, but he leans back.

"Three feet," he says, holding his hands up.

This case warrants an exception. No one jokes about the food I make. I might be small, but I can be fast when I want to be.

Chansol stands at the same moment I do, his hands still up. He should be afraid, because I'm about to give him the beating of a lifetime.

"Please don't," he says, running to the other side of the table. "I promise that was the best thing I've ever tasted."

I fake left then sprint right, but he's made his way around faster.

"I'm sorry," he says, his face turning red. "I won't do it again."

Words aren't going to calm me down, I'm on a mission.

I start to move right, and he moves in the same circle. When he gets to the edge of the table, I pause, taking a good look at him.

"Let's just sit down and eat again," he suggests.

My shoulders go down, and I let my face relax so he thinks I'm giving in. He lowers his hands and takes a deep breath. That's when I jump.

"Three feet!" he screams when I get hold of his hoodie.

I go straight for his armpits. He lets out a high-pitched squeal, and I know I've struck tickling gold.

"Please, please," he begs, but I just get in closer, tickling harder. If he thinks I'm letting him go, he's wrong.

"Time out!" He's out of breath, but I'm having too much fun.

One second, I'm winning, and the next second, I'm on the couch. I was so focused on my torture I didn't consider the retaliation. He's standing over me, hands keeping me from sitting up. He goes for my ribs, and I try to push his hands off. It doesn't work.

Laughter spews from my mouth against my will. I try to get him back—to find the sweet spot I was in before—but his arms are too long.

"Stop!"

"Stop what?" he says with a smirk. "This?"

I'm giggling, but it hurts. "No!"

There's only one way I'm getting out of this. My arms might be too short to tickle him, but his knees are right next to my feet. I hook my toes into the back of his kneecap, and he falls over, right on top of me.

We're nose to nose, out of breath, and searching each other's eyes. In the overcast morning light, he looks like he's been dipped in amber. His pupils widen with desire, the honey color of his eyes barely visible.

"Talitha," he says, his voice lighter than air.

"Yes?"

Powdered sugar has stuck to his lips, and his kiss is sweeter than before. His hands are hot on my back, pulling me closer.

I want to give in. It would be so easy to get lost in the desire. Every inch of me comes alive with his touch. His arms are hard, muscles flexed as he holds onto me. A bit of stubble has grown on his chin, and it feels rough on my cheek.

"Chansol, we can't."

"I know," he says, not kissing but not moving away, either. "I won't."

When I think about it, I start to believe what he said to me last night, that he really does like me. I mean, the boy can't leave me alone.

I press my palms into his chest and give a gentle shove. He gives me one last kiss, right at the corner of my mouth, and stands.

"Three feet," he says again, his voice hoarse. "From now on, I promise."

My laughter still can't be contained, and I lay my head on the arm of the couch. "I think we just need to avoid lying down again."

"You're right," he says, taking my hands and pulling me up. "Let's eat breakfast."

I nod, going back to my seat. He sits next to me, pulling his plate over to my side. His hand rests on my knee.

He digs in, taking big bites of the pancake, not looking at me. I start to eat too, slower than he does.

"This is so good," he says. "I have a new favorite breakfast."

I smile, glad he's enjoying it. As for me, I'm enjoying having him by my side. Watching him eat makes me all warm and gooey inside.

"You're really not leaving, are you?" I say.

He chokes, the back of his hand covering his white-spotted lips. His gaze meets mine, and he coughs for a minute, eyes watering.

"Talitha," he says, once he gets his composure. "If my life was my own, I'd never leave."

#fangirlproblem18

The word bias should be a synonym to pain.

I keep my eyes closed, fighting my drowsy senses as I listen to the soft chatter of the T.V. in the background. Chansol and I must've fallen asleep on the couch, though I don't remember when.

"Now to our Korean correspondent, Nana, with a story about a Korean boy band visiting us here in Houston."

My brow wrinkles as I pinch my eyelids tighter. Nana. Why is it that I don't like that name?

"Fans gather outside NRG Stadium, eagerly awaiting the popular group X-O. But a mystery surrounds one of the members. After   rumors of one of the boys dating, Chansol Park has gone missing."

My eyelids pop open. It's that witch. The one who was there at the hotel, trying to get a gossip scoop from me. I hate her.

"Although representatives claim Mr. Park is fine, there's been no proof to back up their statements. Fans, both here and abroad, are making signs and holding candles to show their support for the beloved member of the boy band."

I search the couch for the remote. Mostly, I just want something to throw at the screen, but I also want to turn it off before I hear another word.

The second I press the power button, the sound of the television is replaced with the sound of screams. I cover my ears and stand.

"What's going—" It's Sam. She's standing in the doorway, mouth open, and designer bag carelessly dropped to the ground.

She stops screaming for a second, and then starts up again. I follow her gaze to Chansol who's just outside the bathroom, brushing his teeth. I'm not sure where he got the toothbrush from, but he's also wearing an I heart New York tee-shirt, so I'm guessing he did a little shopping— although I have no idea where he got money.

Also, not sure where you can find a t-shirt like that in Texas, but it's cool.

"Calm down," I say, running to Sam and taking her shoulders.

Sam is gasping. "Why is he in our house?"

I'm still trying to kick off the sleep. "I didn't think you were coming back today?"

"It's already early evening, the rain stopped," she says, crossing her arms.

Oh. I guess I slept a long time; it was just so nice in Chansol's arms.

106

Sam stamps her foot and points to Chansol. "You didn't answer my question."

Oh gosh, Chansol's here and I fell asleep on him. I know now that he's going to hold onto me, but he still has to physically leave me for the concert tomorrow.

I cross the room and stand between the two of them, surprised at how huge Sam's eyes have gone. There's no doubt she knows who he is, but I still feel the need to introduce her. "Sam," I say in English. "This is Chansol. From X-O."

Sam's face has gone tomato red. An arm reaches over my shoulder as Chansol extends his hand to shake. His abs are pressing into my back. I can tell Sam's thinking about Chansol spending the night here. Chansol rests his chin on my shoulder, putting his free hand around my middle.

Great. That clears everything right up.

I feel him leave and hear the bathroom door shut. Sam grabs both my arms, the goofiest grin on her face. "What the heck happened? I kept trying to call you again, but you didn't answer, and no one was picking up the hall phone."

I'm still kind of high from Chansol's touch. I give her a lazy smirk. "I had to leave my phone at work because of the paparazzi."

Sam flips. "Paparazzi?!"

I try to hush her, but I realize Chansol might not understand her anyway since she's speaking English.

Chansol comes out of the bathroom and drapes an arm over my shoulders. I freeze. He gives me a squeeze, pulling me closer to him.

I look up and he's smiling at me. He leans down and kisses my cheek. "Morning, babe," he whispers in my ear.

Giggles bubble out of my mouth. I can't help it. I'm a total sucker around him. I hope I don't have circles under my eyes. Pretty sure I smell like B.O., too. I've been in the same clothes since last night.

"I'm going to take a shower," I say in English, hoping he understands. "Just...talk."

Yeah right, like they even can. Chansol spins me around before I can walk out of his embrace and gives me a tight hug. "You're cute when you sleep," he says.

So embarrassing. I can't leave fast enough. It was fine when we were alone, but in front of Sam... I haven't had a chance to explain everything yet.

Time for another speed shower and dressing. I don't want to waste time being away from Chansol.

When I come out, they're sitting across the table from each other. Chansol is back to eating the cold pizza, while Sam stares at him like she's feeding a lost puppy.

I sit next to Sam and link my arm through hers. "How are you doing?" I try to speak slowly for Chansol's sake.

"Did you guys sleep together?" Sam says really loud.

Wow, she doesn't waste any time. Technically, the answer is yes, but I know what she really means. "No," I reply. "Chansol's a gentleman."

Sam has a guilty smirk on her face. What on earth is she thinking? "So...how did this happen, then?"

"Samantha," Chansol says suddenly, shocking both of us. "Samantha, Sam. Yep."

That was strange.

"*Bangapsumida*," Chansol says, standing and bowing to Sam.

Sam bows back, and it's adorably awkward. Chansol winks at her and gives her a thumbs-up.

What the heck is that about?

"Is he okay?" Sam says, leaning sideways to be closer to my ear.

I put my hand in front of my mouth. "I'm not sure."

She nods like it's all cool. "So. Who wants to clean up?"

Typical Sam, thinking about cleaning at a time like this. Wasn't she complaining to me about me not having a man? Now she wants me to clean when we have so little time left?

"Let's go for a walk," I say in Korean, pulling at Chansol's hand.

He laces his fingers with mine and tips his head at Sam. "You awesome."

I try not to laugh at his English attempt, but it's too cute.

He shoots her another thumbs-up as I drag him from the room. Glad to know he likes my roommate.

We skip down the stairs, and I keep catching Chansol looking at me. I wonder if he thinks it's crazy we're together, too. It still doesn't seem real.

He stops me before I open the door outside. "One kiss?" he asks.

How can I say no to those puppy-dog eyes?

He still tastes as good as I remember, all sweet and spicy and just...perfect.

This time he breaks away first, gripping my arms for a silent moment before releasing me. Our hands lace together again before we step out into the evening sun.

I blink a few times. That isn't the sun—they're camera flashes. I'm not sure how it happened, but we're surrounded by paparazzi—and they're all snapping pics of Chansol holding my hand.

Chansol lets go and steps in front of me to try and block my face, but we both know it's too late.

The exact thing we'd tried to avoid earlier happened, but how?

"Chansol!" someone screams.

Actually, a lot of people are screaming for Chansol, but this one voice makes him turn his head. I look up to see Taehyun standing on a lamppost, waving to us. He beckons us to come, another big black van waiting to take us away.

Chansol takes my hand again and says, "Keep your head down."

I do as he commands, but I don't know how much that'll help. We're pushing our way through the crowd, flashes assaulting our eyes. People are trying to separate our hands and I'm terrified. What if they hurt Chansol?

Worse still, I know they all hate me for being with *their* idol. The dislike is palpable, pulsing on my senses. I hear a few reporters shouting questions, asking who I am. I swear, all of them sound like Nana.

The crowd presses in on all sides, squishing me out. I'm so disoriented, so lost in the crowd, and it takes me a minute to understand the situation I'm in. They're calling out for Chansol, not me. They'll never call for me. Why? Because I don't belong in his world.

If the roles were switched between me and the crowd, wouldn't I be the one who's hating the girl Chansol's with? This whole time I've known it's too good to be true.

Early today I felt so sure about us, but now that I'm here, I'm doubting. It's because I'm a fangirl. Trapped in my own bubble had given me rose-colored-glasses, but they've been shattered by the situation. Why do I always let myself get caught up in a dream when I know how the world really works?

He's not going to be around forever. I live here, and he lives on the other side of the world. The crowd is so thick, Chansol's hand starts to slip. I know then what I have to do, because I don't own him. No fan does.

By trying to stay with him, I'll be causing him—and the fans—pain.

As much as I feel for him, as much as I want us to be together, it's not realistic. There's too much fighting against us. This is just the start. If I go with him now, the torture will never end. How can he be happy if he spends all his time protecting me?

It takes less than half a second to release his hand. In that moment, a wall of bodies rises up, blocking me from being with him again.

The last thing I see before the crowd swallows me is Chansol opening his eyes wide, reaching for me. But there are so many people between us now.

Before I know it, I've been spit out from the crowd like chewed gum. The black van starts driving away. A few of the paparazzi turn, trying to take pictures of me, but I'm not going to let them. I dash into the building, up the stairs, and slam the door behind me.

My knees give out, the reality of my choice rushing in quickly. I let him go.

I did it for him, though. He'll be better, happier without me. I'm sure he can find an idol that'll suit him, one that's really deserving of his love.

Time passes, that much I know. Whether it's passing fast or slow doesn't matter. All I know is that each second I sit here, the farther Chansol is from me.

Eventually, Sam is there. Patting my arms and asking if I'm okay.

Okay? What does that mean anyway? Can someone be okay when their world explodes? Chansol and I had one amazing day, and now it's over.

Turns out he wasn't the one who stuck the knife in my heart. It was me.

I've pulled it out with such force I'll probably die from the bleeding, and there's nothing I can do about it.

It's my fault. I was the one who loved Chansol when I knew better. I was the one who let him stay when I could've walked away. I was the one who was selfish enough to let him in when hurting was the only real end.

Me. I'm the one who needs to be sorry. Chansol is innocent.

At least he can move on. He's perfect enough to get any girl he wants.

Jennie Bennett

For one shining moment that girl was me, but it never will be again.

#fangirlproblem19

Crying over a bias is the norm.

"All right," Sam says the next morning. "I have an idea."

Idea? I don't like the sound of that. All I want to do is sit in my sweats, drink tea, and think of Chansol.

"I'm not going to let you mope. We're going out tonight."

That's the last thing I want to do. I need at least a week to recover from everything. There's no one I want to dress up for, anyway.

"You'll want to come, trust me," Sam says.

Yeah, just like she wanted me to go to the store last night for some milk. That all went sour when I saw some baseball caps and thought of Chansol. Crying in the middle of the aisle is not a great way to spend a Saturday night.

I know it was my choice, but it doesn't hurt any less.

Sam slams her hand on the table so I'm forced to look up. "I'm taking away your computer until you get up and come with me."

Like that'll work. I haven't even been online since I left Chansol. Almost twenty-four hours. That has to be a record for me.

Jennie Bennett

I sip my tea until I make annoying slurping sounds, and then I sip some more—looking pointedly at Sam.

"Disgusting," she says, leaving the room. Good. Maybe that'll make her keep her distance.

I am curious, though. I've stayed away from the Internet, so I don't even know if Chansol is okay. Were the pictures of us posted online? What are people saying about them?

The same questions have been going through my mind since yesterday, and I've been too chicken to find out.

If nothing else, I need to check it to put my mind at ease. Then I can start moving on. Maybe I can even quell the rumors. Come out as *that girl* and tell everyone Chansol and I weren't dating. Even though we were. Kind of.

The computer takes forever to load, and I bounce my knee the whole time. Even when the browser opens, it takes a few seconds for anything to show up. Stupid Internet.

I go to Twitter first. If anything is happening, I'll find out there. I scroll through my notifications and don't see a single thing about it.

Is it wrong to be disappointed? I mean, I thought there would be *something*. I didn't even get to take a *selca* with Chansol–which means our time together will only live in my dreams. I can't tell anyone, either. Only Sam knows, and she doesn't care enough to back me up.

Maybe my savvy friends on Twitter just haven't heard yet. Either that or they don't care.

I click on the search bar and type in *Park Chansol* followed by yesterday's date. Yes! An Everythingkpop article. It wasn't totally ignored.

The link pulls up a picture of Chansol—wearing his jeans and my hoodie. He's carrying a shopping bag, and he still has bed head.

Park Chansol was spotted shopping in Houston today, relaxing before his performance tomorrow. The concert is expected....

I don't read the rest because I don't need to. All I know is that someone spotted him when he bought a toothbrush yesterday, and that's probably what brought the paparazzi to my house. If I hadn't fallen asleep, I could've gone to the store for him, and none of this would've happened.

I wonder what it took to block the story about the two of us from leaking. I can't imagine it was easy.

How can I give up on him when he's still trying to protect me from afar? I may have been the one to start this mess, but if he didn't care, he'd let the photos go. If only I could see his face and ask him what he's thinking.

What an idiot I've been. I didn't even get his phone number.

"Sam," I call.

She comes running from her room, slipping a little as she sits across from me.

"I think you're right," I say. "We need to go out tonight."

Sam's eyes go wide. "Really?"

"Yeah, we're going to the X-O concert."

Sam furrows her brow. "We are?"

Even if Chansol rejects me for what I did, I need to give him an apology at least.

"I don't care how long it takes, I'm going to wait until the concert is over. When they come out, I'll see Chansol one last time."

Sam's mouth is a thin line, her big eyes glossed over. "I don't think that's such a good idea. I'm not sure I want to see this side of you again."

"Look," I say, "either you come with me or I go by myself, but I'm going. I've made up my mind."

Sam tightens her jaw but doesn't say anything.

"We can go shopping," I say, my voice rising in pitch at the end of the sentence. Sam loves shopping. Nothing gets her out of the house like the thought of new clothes.

She pouts. "Will you let me pick your outfit?"

As much as I hate to admit it, Sam has better taste than I do. I normally look amazing in whatever she chooses. "Sure."

"And do your makeup at Sephora?"

That's pushing it. She normally likes to do this dark dramatic stuff on me, which is not my style. But I'll admit it makes me look sexy. I really need Sam to support me, so I'm not going to let a little vanity get in my way.

If Chansol really likes me, he'll like me for who I am. He already saw me at my worst. "Fine."

Sam squeals and pulls me out of the kitchen chair. After I shower, she asks to do my hair, too. If it's fun for her, then I don't have a problem with it.

My hair is about shoulder length, and most of the time it's pulled back since I'm in the kitchen. I also find it totally unmanageable. Sam uses some weird products then spends forever with a hot curling iron to my head, but when I turn around, I gasp.

My brown hair is in perfect glossy curls. I didn't even know it could do that.

We hit the mall next. Sam picks out this super tight red dress, but it looks amazing on me. She offers to pay for everything since I still don't have my purse back. I'm starting to feel worthy of a Kpop star.

Jennie Bennett

The only thing I refuse to let her do to me is wear heels. I consent to strappy sandals, but I'm planning on being on my feet for a long time. Heels are just crazy.

By the time we leave the mall—Sephora bags in our hands—I actually have guys turning their heads to look at me. Can't say that's ever happened before. Sorry, boys, I'm taken. At least I hope I'm taken.

We arrive at the venue before the concert starts. People are cramming their way inside, wearing X-O shirts and blaring songs from their phones. I don't know why I wanted to be here so early. I'm hoping for a miracle...someone to give me their ticket or something.

I should know better. If any of these fans are like me—and I'm guessing most of them are—they wouldn't give up their ticket unless someone murdered them.

"Let's go wait by the stage door," I say to Sam once the doors are closed and the music has started.

Sam groans. "Let's get something to eat instead. I'm starved."

No way, I'm not giving up now that I'm here. I'm on a hunger strike until the night is over. Food is my favorite thing in the world, but it can't compare to Chansol.

Some big burly dudes are standing around the back door and not letting anyone come near. We're not the only girls trying to get in.

I look around and spot an apartment building across from us. If we could just get to the top, we could watch from the big screens since the building's roof is open.

"No," Sam says when I suggest the idea. "I'm hungry."

"I let you dress me up," I say, stomping.

Her lower lip juts out. "You didn't let me buy you those fabulous heels."

Is she still hung up on that?

"How about this: you grab something at the convenience store across the street and meet me at the roof of the apartment."

She brightens. "Okay! Anything you want?"

"I don't care," I say. I just want to see the concert.

Sam skips off, and I'm faced with the mission of getting inside.

I wait, one foot pressed to the wall, head down, until someone comes out.

People have done this in movies a hundred times, looking all smooth and walking up to the door like it's not a big deal, but I'm shaking. I squeak out a nervous "hi" to the person leaving. They look at me funny but leave without a word.

I stride inside, trying to act like I own the place in case someone is watching. Then I run back to the door and shove some paper from the trashcan under the doorjamb so it doesn't shut all the way, but it's not noticeable.

My feet aren't moving to the top floor as quickly as I need them to. All right, so I take the elevator, but it still seems like *for-ev-er*. I end up going around the top hall a few hundred times before I spot the exit to the roof.

I have to pull down some stairs to get there, and they creak loudly as I do so. I leave them open so Sam can find me easier.

Just as I've hoped, the view is perfect. The giant screens show all the boys' faces. Every time the cameras pan to Chansol, I let out a scream. It's not like anyone can hear me with the amount of wind blowing up here, but I can't help myself.

This dress was a dumb idea because I'm freezing.

The pounding that comes from the stadium can barely be heard over the howling wind. I don't care. It's worth it. And at the end of the night, I'll get to see Chansol again. Then I can fix everything. I'm going to tell him I'm crazy about him. I'm going to let him hold me, and I'm going to figure out a way to be with him. Even if we're separated by thousands of miles.

I hear someone coming up the stairs and I'm actually glad, because I'm hungrier than I first let on.

"Sam!" I say, turning my head.

But it's not Sam. It's not anyone I know. Scratch that—it's someone I know. Someone I know very well.

It's that witch of a reporter, Nana.

I have no idea how she found me, but I can't really think about it. My attention is glued to the big screen. Not because of Chansol, but because I can see my own face staring back at me.

Jennie Bennett

#fangirlproblem20

A true fangirl never gives up.

"It was you, wasn't it?" Nana asks, trying to block my view of the stadium.

I ignore her, shoving around her to get a better look. Some video is playing of me. A video I've never seen before. Since I'm in the video, I remember all the occasions. There was a week a few months back when Sam was filming me on her phone each opportunity she could get. I didn't understand then, and I don't understand now. Why is it playing on the stadium screen?

"You know," Nana says, "I can call the police if you'd like, or you can talk to me."

I still don't know how she found me, or why she cares. So what if I was with Chansol? It's not her business. Besides, that's all over now.

Except...except...why am I on that screen? I have to know. I have to find Chansol again, I just don't know how.

"What do you want from me?" I ask, finding my voice.

Nana gives a brisk, bark-like laugh, smoothing down one of her stray black hairs. "I think you know. Either you can tell me what happened, or I can make up my own story."

I wouldn't put it past her. She can't know the truth, not until I can talk to Chansol again. If he wants to tell, fine, but it's not my story to give

"How did you find me, anyway?" I say, trying to talk around the subject.

Nana's perfect pink lips pinch together. "Do you think bringing down those stairs, then stomping and yelling on the roof went unnoticed? Someone called the police, and I happened to be in the area. I'm saving you from imprisonment, so you better fess up. What's your connection to Chansol Park?"

It was an accident. The whole thing. Our escape. Us, alone in my apartment. His heavy lips on mine. Me letting go of his hand. None of it should've happened. It was almost like...fate.

I take a deep breath, the reality of the situation twisting my stomach in knots. I have to get to Chansol, now more than ever. If I can see his face and tell him how sorry I am, maybe it could be more. If I try again, it won't be our circumstance that brought us together. If I find him and tell him how I feel, maybe he'll take me back.

Do I dare hope? It's not like I have a choice. Either I go for it now, or forever ask myself *what if*?

"All right," I say, formulating a plan to get off this roof. I don't know what I'll do after that, but I need to do something. "I'll tell you everything. Just...can we go someplace warmer? And quieter?"

Nana pulls her smartphone from her pocket and hits a button. She was trying to record our conversation. I knew it.

"Works for me. The studio van should be nice and cozy."

Great, now I just have to figure out how to get away from her.

I charge ahead, but she stops me.

"Not so fast," she says, hooking my elbow until our arms are connected. "We should walk like this. You know, so I can trust you."

Riigght. Or keep me from getting away.

"Now tell me," she says once we're in the quiet elevator. "How did you kidnap Chansol Park?"

Kidnapped? She saw him drive over to get me, not the other way around. But I know she'll use my words against me, so it's better not to talk. "Cranberries," I say, hedging.

Nana startles. "What?"

"You had cranberries for dinner, I can smell it all over your breath. I think I have some gum in my purse if you'd like a stick." I hold up my clutch so she can see. She'd have to let go of me if I were to open it and search inside.

"Uh," she says, covering her mouth as she speaks. "No thanks. I think I have some mints in the van."

Dang. It was worth a shot, anyway.

She pushes the button again, even though the elevator is already moving. I guess she wants to get to the bottom soon.

We exit arm in arm as I keep calculating. She's in heels, and I'm in flats, so I have a decent chance of outrunning her. But if I shove her to the ground, what will she say on the news?

The situation worsens after we open the apartment doors. All of the vans that were in front of the hotel are back, a whole crowd of people waiting to see what I have to say.

My eyes scan the area, looking for any escape. Just when I'm about to lose hope, salvation comes into my line of sight. Dark hair, killer body, and two gas-station sandwiches in her hands.

Sam.

I'm not sure how she got around the reporters, but she can be surprisingly sneaky when she wants to be.

The words "Help me!" are screaming inside my head, but I'm not sure Sam can see me well enough to understand my expression.

"I want to make a statement right here," I tell Nana, planting my feet.

She balks for a moment but settles when I keep my mouth a straight line. Her phone comes out of her pocket again, and she holds the microphone part to my mouth.

"What would you like to tell us...uh...what's your name?"

"My name is Talitha," I say loudly. "And I have a confession to make."

Nana looks like she has me cornered now, a smirk twisting her perfectly powdered features. "Go on, I'm listening."

I take one look at the place Sam was standing, but she's not there anymore. I hope she got the hint.

"My name is Talitha," I say again. "And I'm a fangirl."

Nana looks confused for a second, so I continue on.

"Yes, I love Chansol. Not just like, but *love*. Really, really love him." My voice cracks on the words, and Nana looks pleased with herself. "But," I add in near whisper, "so do the thousands of other fans in that stadium. I love Chansol all on my own, and I'll keep loving him, even if he never loves me back. That's what it means to be a fangirl."

Nana's grip on my arm loosens, her mouth hanging open, her eyebrows raised. I can see it all in that one look. She knows. She's been a fangirl, and she understands. I wonder if that's the reason she so aggressively pursued the story in the first place.

"Excuse me," Sam says, appearing behind Nana, still holding the sandwiches in her hands.

Nana, who now has tears in her eyes, turns around. I guess my speech was that moving.

Sam gives her a small smile. "Sorry, but I'm gonna need you to hold these."

For half a second, I'm just as surprised as Nana. Reflexively, Nana drops my arm to hold the sandwiches, and Sam jerks my wrist–trailing me away.

I don't know if it's my imagination, or simply the wind playing tricks in my ears. But I swear I hear Nana wishing me good luck.

It doesn't take long for my reflexes to kick in, and I start running with Sam at my toes. Now's the time. I have to get to Chansol or I may never see him again.

We play *Frogger* across the busy road, and I pass Sam up as we get close to the back entrance of the stadium. I look for an opening and see a few girls distracting a guard. Perfect for me.

I finally have my chance to make something of myself, and I'm going for it.

In my head, I can see everything behind me. No doubt those cops noticed us jaywalking, and now I'm about to take on breaking and entering for the second time tonight. This should be fun.

I run straight past the first guard, but the second one makes a grab at me. Sam is right there, throwing her shoe at the back of the guard's head.

"Run, Talitha, run!" Sam screams. She's going to stay behind and wrestle my demons for me.

There's one more burly guy in black standing right at the stage entrance. For once, I'm glad I'm short. I fake left then dodge right, slipping under his arms. The backstage staff scream and move out of the way as I pump my legs.

Sprinting is the wrong word for it. I'm flat out flying.

I make it to the stage, heart pumping. Chansol is in the middle of rapping to *Overdone*. All the members are around him, keeping me from getting in.

I bowl them over, anyway. A few of them take hold of my dress. I push forward with all my strength. Security guards converge, the screens going black. The music cuts off and the fans roar. Chansol's name screeches from my throat.

"I'm sorry!!" I'm yelling, my cries getting drowned out by the crowd. "Chansol!!"

There are too many hands. It's too dark. It's too loud. It's too much. I made one stupid mistake and now I'll never see him again.

"I'm sorry," I whisper again, my eyes welling. "And I love you."

It's a cry only I can hear. A song for myself, the person who'll always be alone. Because there's only one man for me and I'll never be able to touch him.

Jennie Bennett

#fangirlproblem21

Not knowing when to quit.

The lights flick back on as I'm getting carried off the stage. I lean forward with all my might, staring at Chansol—willing him to see me.

He's almost out of my vision when I hear him yell, "Wait!"

Could it be?

The hands are still dragging me away, but I start screaming again. "Chansol!"

Fans are shouting, but this time it's with cheers of joy. "Talitha!" My name rings out over the dome, a microphone turned on to blare the noise from Chansol's mouth over the crowd.

All my fight rushes to me, the monster breaking free of its cage. It's not a fangirl monster anymore, but one who would fight to keep someone she loves in her life.

With a single primal roar, I break away from the hands, and back toward Chansol. He's running for me as well, his face breaking into the biggest smile I've seen.

I don't care how many people are watching, he's all mine.

We collide—space, time, people...none of them matter. It's just me and him, spinning in our own axis.

He doesn't waste time, and neither do I. As we embrace, my lips smash into his. Both his arms grip my middle and he spins me around as I hold his face. Confetti rains down on us, and I catch our giant forms on the big screen. To heck with fame, to heck with prying eyes. I'm never letting Chansol go.

***

As if X-O singing to me wasn't enough, as if Chansol getting on one knee during the rap didn't make me whole, I get to wait for them backstage. Me and Sam.

The boys made an agreement with the reporters so the story is staying quiet. Now the only thing I'm doing is staying close to my boyfriend.

I get a little giddy thinking of the word *boyfriend*, knowing what it means. It means Chansol and I are together, for real, and nothing can stop that unless we choose to stop it. Which I won't. Lesson learned.

"Your boyfriend is pretty hot," Sam says, watching the concert from backstage.

I'm munching on a pretzel, swinging my legs because I'm so happy. Happy's not even a strong enough word. Nothing is.

The encore ends, and all the members join us in the greenroom.

Chansol puts his arms around me and I lean into his chest. I don't care how sweaty he is, that's *my* sweat.

He nuzzles my neck and I giggle. "I'm so glad you're back," he whispers in my ear. "They wouldn't let me see you again, and I didn't have your phone number."

"I'm sorry I left," I say, rubbing my hands down his arms.

"Hey, I went to great lengths to stay with you. I even pretended I didn't have money for a hotel."

I swat at him, not believing he just made that confession

He ignores my attempt to punish him and pulls me close again. "What matters is that we're together."

I turn around to face him, and get lost in his eyes, taking in every detail—not so I can save it for later, but so I can cherish it now.

He kisses me, the deep cinnamon scent filling my nose.

"Get a room!" someone yells.

Popcorn hits my side, but we don't stop. We're together again, and they need to give us a moment.

"Well, that's disgusting," Sam says.

All right, now it's ruined. I'm laughing as I pull away, Chansol still holding onto my waist.

"Did you see the video?" he says. "Is that why you came?"

I'm not sure what the deal was with that. "Yeah, but I didn't hear anything. I was on the roof across the street."

Chansol looks at my roommate. "Sam. Samantha. Sam."

I raise an eyebrow at her. "You made that video, didn't you?"

Her cheeks go red. "Yeah, I did."

"How?" I say, looking between the two of them.

"Twitter and Instagram," Chansol says. "I saw all of your comments on Instagram, and Sam sent me the video on Twitter every day. Most of the time, I ignore stuff like that, but her words seemed so genuine, I finally clicked play."

"And?" I say, wondering what Chansol thought.

He faces me again. "I fell for you right away. Never thought I'd get to meet you, though."

Ha! I could say the same thing about him. "So, when you saw me at the hotel?"

"I made my company book your hotel. But when I saw you, I didn't know what to do," he admits. "I thought I could start a conversation by giving you the picture, but then you started crying."

I cover my face with my hands. Maybe it's a good thing, but I feel like an idiot for doing that now.

"I had hinted to the media that I liked someone. I didn't name names, and that's why the paparazzi came.

They never wrote a story because they had nothing to go on."

My breath hitches in my chest. This can't be real.

"The way I see it," Chansol says, "Fate pushed us together. So what if the media caught us? At least we're here now."

I peek between my fingers. "What did you put in that video, Sam?"

Sam smiles. "How about we all watch it together?"

Chansol doesn't let me leave. Since there's not enough room for all three of us on the loveseat, I end up sitting in his lap and watching the video on Sam's phone over her shoulder.

"Hi!" Sam says, hangul characters translating her words. "I want to tell you about a friend of mine. She's just an ordinary girl." The scene changes from Sam to me. It's a shot of us getting ice cream together, and me spooning it onto my tongue like a derp.

Next, it shows me in the kitchen, working with my head down, whisking some meringue. Maybe that's what Chansol meant when he mentioned a whisk on the phone back at my apartment.

"She likes tea." A few shots go by of me drinking my daily dose. "She's obsessed with sneakers." A full pan view of my overflowing closet. "And the best thing about her is that she loves you."

There's a scene I don't remember Sam filming of me in a hoodie, staring at pictures of Chansol. No wonder he didn't react when he saw me doing the same thing back in the apartment.

"Her name is Talitha, and she saved my life once." Next, there's a picture of me spinning around at an amusement park, a smile on my face. "When I thought I was worthless, she was the friend who lifted me up." Another frame of me dancing around the living room, trying to do the moves to an X-O song and failing, but laughing it off, anyway. "It took me a while," Sam's voice says, "but I figured it out. It's because you taught her how to smile." One last picture of Chansol smiling before everything fades to black. "I wanted to thank you, and her, for being amazing people."

Chansol squeezes me tighter, and I know Sam's words are right. I may have saved her life, but she saved mine, too. Now I get to spend the rest of forever with the person I love.

Jennie Bennett

#*fan*GIRLFRIEND**problem**1

The other biases.

"You know his feet smell, right?" Chansol says, looking over my shoulder. I have a picture open of Minji from PTS, and he is looking *fine*.

Every time Chansol catches me gushing over another man, he has something to say. I'm not swayed by it. He knew I had this problem for a while, and honestly, I know he's teasing.

"Feet can be washed," I deadpan, still scrolling through.

Chansol sits on the coffee table and scoots my laptop over so I can't reach the mouse. "And he has a girlfriend."

I tilt my head as I stare at him. "As do you, but that doesn't stop you from posting pictures online."

He clicks his teeth together, narrowing his eyes. "Maybe, but it's my job."

I reach forward and pat his hand. "You're so cute when you're jealous."

He turns out of my grip, folding his arms and pouting. His bottom lip is incredibly sexy like that.

"*Oppa*," I say, pulling out my best *aegyo*. I slide over on the couch so he can see me better. "*Saranghae*," I add, Korean for *I love you*. I throw him little hearts with my crossed finger and thumbs.

He lifts his chin up, looking at the ceiling.

"*Oppa*," I try again, laying on the cuteness as thick as I can. "*Heartu*? Love?" I continue, making another heart out of my hands then putting my arms above my head and my fingertips to my scalp to make a bigger heart.

He crosses his arms tighter, still huffing.

There's only one thing to cure this anger. I stand, moving in front of him. Placing my palms flat on the table, I trap him between my arms.

"*Oppa*," I whisper near his ear. "*Ppoppo*?" Asking for a kiss.

He glances at me, and I bat my eyelashes the best I can. His lips press together, but I can see the corners of his mouth going up in a smile. I almost have him.

"*Ppoppo* here?" I ask, quickly kissing his cheek. His arms stay crossed. "*Ppoppo* here?" I say again, smacking my lips on his forehead. He loosens up a little, but not enough. "*Ppoppo*...here?" My tone turns seductive as I lean in for his lips.

He grabs my face as our mouths meet, giving me a deep, meaningful, kiss. Man, I love this guy.

I can hardly believe it's been a year since we got together. And that I was able to finish culinary school in Korea and get a good job. Really, my life is a dream come true.

We're no longer kissing, but Chansol is still holding onto my face, his cinnamon breath tickling my nose.

"You know you're the only guy for me," I say, stealing one more quick kiss.

"I know," he says. "But I still want you all to myself."

I sit on his lap, wrapping my arms around his waist and laying my head on his chest. "Those other guys, none of them hold a candle to you—never have. They can be the most attractive guy in the world, but they'll only be looks. To me, you're everything."

I squeeze him tighter, and he puts his arms around me. "If you don't want me to look," I continue, "I'll stop. But when I see another guy like that, I'm only reminded of how much I love you. You're it for me."

"Wow," he says, moving to stand.

"What?" I ask. "Did I do something wrong?"

He visibly swallows, eyes closed. "No."

"Then what?"

He reaches in his pocket and pulls something out. I can't see since his hands are huge and he's holding it tightly.

"The problem is," he says, "you took the words right out of my mouth."

I smile. He can be so corny sometimes, but I love it.

140

He scratches the back of his neck like he's nervous. "I was going to save this for later, but..." He gets down on one knee.

Both my hands go over my mouth, eyes about to pop out of my head.

"I'm sorry this isn't fancy," he says, "but I couldn't wait a minute longer."

His fingers move just enough for me to see a box, Tiffany blue. I'm shaking. This cannot be happening.

"The truth is, I've always known you're the girl of my dreams. When we met, I knew right away. You're the girl I want to spend forever with."

I'm crying now, huge teardrops rolling down my face.

"So, what do you say? Will you be my wife?"

I shake my head with a resounding yes but can't seem to produce the word. But that's the thing about us, I don't have to say it. He already knows.

He stands, coaxing my left hand from my face so he can slide a ring on my finger. He kisses me despite the tears, and I can feel his love emanating so huge it could fill the world.

This is it. Chansol is my forever. And I can't think of a better person to have by my side.

If you loved this book, please leave a review!

Fangirl Problems

Jennie Bennett

Acknowledgements

This is always the hardest part of writing a book since there's not enough thanks in the world to all the people who have helped me with my books. And the order of how they're mentioned here doesn't in any way change how much impact they've made on me and this book.

Of course, I'll start with the real Talitha. Thanks for your name and for your love of a certain Kpop star whose name starts with Chan. It's your fault he's on my bias list, too. Meanie.

I always have to mention my husband first as he's the main influence for my leading men. He didn't mind kissing me when I was looking to get descriptions just right, and he's my first go-to when I need to brainstorm aloud. Girls, wait to get yourself a guy who will respect and love you. There are good men out there, and my husband is proof.

Next, I have to mention my mother. I'm tearing up as I write this because she's been such a huge support to me. Thank you, Mom, for always buying my books and telling your friends about them. And thank you for taking me to Korea with you. It was an experience I'll never forget.

A huge thanks to all the girls in KDA who constantly support and uplift me when I'm down. I love the Kdrama games we play and how we can fangirl over shows together. You ladies rock my socks off! There's too many to mention, or else I would put all 200+ of you in here.

Thank you to my Beta Book Peeps, my biggest writing support and those who hear me gripe the most. Cassie Mae, Jenny Morris, Suzi Retzlaff, Theresa Marie, Kelley Gerschke, Rachel Schieffelbein, Jessica Salyer, Lizzy Charles, Leigh Covington, and Hope Roberson, thanks for putting up with me and not kicking me out.

A big thanks to Kim Woodruff for editing this first on such short notice and within a quick timeframe. You've made this book stronger.

I wouldn't be here without the best editor in the world, Precy Larkins. She always makes time for me when I spring editing on her last minute. You are such an incredible, beautiful, person and I love you to death. Thanks for not only being a kick-A editor, but a great friend who has my back. Hugs to you, girl!

To Erica Laurie for teaching me the basics of self-pub and for stepping up as my copyeditor. I really would be doing all of this blind without you. Love you so much!

Without question, I have to give this to my Heavenly Father. I'm grateful he gave me this gift, but also recently reminded me that I still have value without my writing, and that the most important thing is to care for the people around me. My true strength is in being his daughter, and no one can take that away from me.

Last, I have to give my thanks to the most important people who made this book possible: the readers! I'm grateful to everyone who purchases or opens these books. I love to hear from y'all and it makes my day to see new reviews. Please, if you can only leave a review as short as one sentence, it makes all the difference to authors everywhere. Even if it's not for my book, review an author you love to show them how much they mean to you!

Jennie Bennett

About the Author

Jennie Bennett is a mother to four beautiful and crazy children, and wife to a handsome and kind husband. She found a passion in Korean pop culture in January of 2013 and she's never looked back since. She currently resides in Houston, Texas with her husband, kids, and a cute puppy named Charlie.

Twitter: @jabennettwrites

Facebook: Jennie Bennett

Instagram: @jenniefire

Join my newsletter and get free books!

https://www.subscribepage.com/b3f6u5

Fangirl Problems

Jennie Bennett